W9-BHZ-128

Jess
and the
Runaway
Grandpa

Jess
and the
Runaway
Grandpa

Mary Woodbury

COTEAU BOOKS

Edited by Barbara Sapergia.

Cover painting by Ward Schell.
Cover design by Ed Pas.
Typeset by Dik Campbell.
Printed and bound in Canada.

Lyric excerpts on pages 54 and 203 of "You'll Never Walk Alone" by Richard Rodgers and Oscar Hammerstein II, © 1945 Williamson Music. Copyright Renewed. International Copyright Secured. Used by Permission. All Rights Reserved.

The publisher gratefully acknowledges the financial assistance of the Saskatchewan Arts Board, the Canada Council, the Department of Canadian Heritage, and the City of Regina Arts Commission.

Canadian Cataloguing in Publication Data

Woodbury, Mary, 1935-
Jess and the runaway grandpa
ISBN 1-55050-113-5
I. Alzheimer's disease - Juvenile Fiction.   I. Title
PS8595.0644J47 1997   jC813'.54   C96-920011-3
PZ7.W8596Je 1997

COTEAU BOOKS
401-2206 Dewdney Avenue
Regina, Saskatchewan
S4R 1H3

I dedicate this book to Greg and Janelle Caldwell, and the thousands of children who know first-hand what it is like to lose a grandparent to Alzheimer's.

TABLE OF CONTENTS

1. Orange Socks

The day after her cat Midas died Jessie Baines put on a pair of orange socks. It didn't matter that they didn't match her bright purple track suit or her lime green sportsbag or her worn white sneakers with purple laces. What mattered was remembering Midas.

Midas had been one terrific pet. A ball of golden fuzz when they had picked him up at the SPCA, he had grown into an impressive giant. On that first day when the kitten's tiny, sharp, pins-and-needles claws had kneaded Jess's arm leaving marks, her dad had chuckled, "That kitten has the Midas touch. He changes everything he touches."

"But my arm hasn't turned to gold, Daddy," Jess had retorted, being a lippy six year old at the time. Now, six years later, Midas, the huge

1

purring orange machine, had been run over by a speeding half-ton, and would only live in Jess's memory. That's where her dad lived too. He'd moved East shortly after Midas had arrived.

Jess and her mom, Naomi Baines, held a memorial service for the cat in the back yard by the cedar deck. The vet gave them Midas's remains in a Cougar winter boots box. Ernie and Ruth Mather, their old friends from next door, and Brian Dille and his dad Sonny, from down the street, came to the funeral.

Everyone shared stories of Midas except Ernie, who was losing his memory. He stood silent, grey head bowed, rocking back and forth slightly, humming a hymn. Ruth had a black bulky sweater wrapped around her sturdy compact body. Her arthritis complained on damp days.

"Remember how he chased magpies in the yard," Ruth sniffed. "Caught some, too."

Jess could remember showing Midas off proudly to the Mathers when she was young. They'd made a big fuss of her and the cat. They always had. Back then she'd called them Grandma and Grandpa. Her real ones were distant in more ways than miles, as her mom said. The Mathers had adopted all of them. Especially after the Bainses had bought the house next door.

"The firemen had to rescue him from Mathers' elm tree once," Brian added. "He was not a damsel but just dismal in distress."

Jess glared at Brian from under lowered eyelids. Couldn't the clown be serious for one minute?

"He had the loudest purr of all the cats on the block," Sonny Dille sighed.

"He loved green olives." Naomi shoveled clay and sand onto the boot box. The dirt thudded on the cardboard. The smell of damp, turned earth and early crabapple blossoms filled the air. Jess squeezed her stinging eyes shut and pictured Midas eating olives.

"Without the pits," Jess sighed.

They sang "Memories" from the musical *Cats*. Naomi led the chorus with her husky alto voice. Tears made two thin rivers down her plump cheeks. She wiped them away leaving a smudge of dirt on her chin. Jess was tempted to take a Kleenex, dampen it, and wash her mother's face for her. Naomi cared so much for every living thing. She worked too hard, Ruth Mather said. That's why Jess had to be a big girl and help. Answer the phone, take messages, make sure Naomi ate good food. One of Jess's friends at school had said she envied Jess because she had a mom that was more like a big sister who loved pets, and lots of moms didn't.

Poor Midas. Everything Jess thought about reminded her of the cat.

"What are we celebrating?" Ernie's white hair blew in the stiff May breeze. He was wearing his blue windbreaker and matching polyester blue pants. Silver-rimmed glasses perched on his long pale nose. A grey stubble of a beard sprouted on his prominent chin. His cheeks were smooth and pink, but his neck and hands were wrinkled. He had too much skin for the size of his skeleton. Never a big man, Ernie had shrunk since he retired — either that or Jess had grown really fast.

Jess shivered like someone was walking on her grave. Poor Ernie, he'd been like a grandpa, a really great grandpa. Now he was more like a kid. It scared her when he didn't remember who she was. She wanted to scream at him when he did dumb things. Jess's eyes filled with tears. She took the cat's stuffed mouse with its chewed tail and missing eye out of her pocket and tossed it onto the cat's coffin. Everyone else threw some earth into the hole. Her mother planted a rosebush, the sweat joining the tears and the smudges of clay on her flushed face. They all hugged each other, except for Brian and Jess. The two of them stood awkwardly for a moment, hands by their sides. Jess cried silently, mopping her tears with a hankie that Ruth had passed her.

"Midas had a great life." Ruth patted Jess's hand. "He died running. I don't think he would have wanted it any other way."

"It's been a purr-fect afternoon for an interment," Brian said. "Too bad Grandpa Ernie missed it all." He rolled his eyes skyward. Jess wanted to bop him on the head. What an insensitive clod he'd turned out to be.

She couldn't talk as they filed into the house for tea, cheese and crackers, and green olives without the pits. She couldn't say that it wasn't just for Midas she was crying. It was for Ernie and maybe a little for herself. It was as if one bad thing happening reminded her of every other bad thing that had ever happened. Human beings were "complicated critters," like Grandpa Ernie had said when he was a proper grownup.

After everyone left Jess went upstairs and ransacked her dresser until she found the orange socks. She'd only worn them a few times, because they were so loud. Her mother bought them for gymnastics cool-downs and they were loose and baggy and wrinkled and soft and wonderful. Bright and cheerful, like Midas. Jess didn't want to forget Midas. She wouldn't forget him if she wore these socks.

The next morning Jess sat on the front porch waiting for the school bus. The chill from last night's frost seeped through her oversized blue-jean jacket and jeans. She shivered. The smell of wet earth and rotting vegetation filled the air. Spring was taking a long time coming.

Jess pushed a long strand of blond hair out of her blue-green eyes and bent to pull the orange socks up her skinny freckled legs and over the bottom of her jeans. One of her bony elbows cracked. Her lime-green-and-black sportsbag lay open beside her.

"I never saw a kid who carried so much

garbage," her mom said as she locked the front door. "Isn't that bag getting heavy? What is it — your arctic survival kit?"

"I don't like surprises." I wouldn't talk, Mom, about carrying too much stuff, Jess thought, eyeing her mother's overflowing briefcase.

"Didn't I see you putting a sewing kit in there this morning? A sewing kit? I've never seen you sew anything in your life."

"That hunchbacked old lady that always sings 'You are my sunshine' gave it to me. She thanked me for being a good nurse."

"That's Mabel Teasdale. She's ninety-nine." Naomi Baines worked for Home Care Services in Edmonton. Saturdays Jess went with her to visit the local Seniors lodge. Naomi loved all her old people. She often visited the frail ones she had helped when they could still live on their own. She liked to ease their transition to living in an institution, she said. Loyalty ranked high on Jess's mom's list of priorities. It made Jess feel pretty secure.

"What a funny kid!" Naomi shook her frizzy blond hair and tied an escaping purple-patterned scarf around her throat. She reached down with her chubby arm, picked up her brimming briefcase, and headed for the garage. "What's with the wild orange socks? They don't match anything else you've got on."

Mom didn't wait for an answer. If Naomi Baines had a bumper sticker on her old green Volvo it would read, "Have you bugged your kid today?" Jess chewed her lip, peered down the street watching for the bus.

She reached into her sportsbag for some gum, humming a few bars from "Memories." One side pocket had first aid supplies — band-aids, gauze, mosquito repellent, sunscreen, scissors, nail file, tweezers, and burn, bite, and sore muscle ointments. Now old Miss Teasdale's sewing kit was nestled in there too. The other side pocket had food supplies: gum (two flavours, cinnamon and peppermint), candy bars, cough drops, fruit strips, and granola bars. In the front pocket she had a compass and a Swiss Army knife that her dad had left behind, a pen, pencil, pencil sharpener, and a pad of paper. Her notebook and Math text were inside. She unwrapped a stick of peppermint gum, folded it in half, and popped it in her mouth.

A continuous line of traffic flowed along the Whitemud Drive, the freeway half a block away. The man across the street scraped ice from his windshield. Brian Dille stood at the other end of the block tapping his left foot impatiently, waiting for the school bus. His black numbered T-shirt, sweat pants, and tawny skin made him look like a short football player. His dad came from one of the Caribbean islands, his mom from some small town outside of Calgary. A black curly mop of hair covered Brian's head. His sparkling black eyes hardly showed under the heap of hair. Too bad he had turned into such a clown, such a dummy. This year he had started hanging out with the bullies and macho midgets in their class. He giggled like a maniac every time one of them managed to tease a girl or made a fuss in the classroom. Jess had let him come to Midas's funeral for old times' sake, that was all. Even then he had to open his big mouth.

The school bus pulled around the corner and stopped for Brian. Jess sighed, thinking of old times, collected her bag and started down the walk. Just then the side door of the Mather house burst open.

"David? Yvonne, where are you? It's time for school, kids." Ernie Mather hollered in the direction of the street and then turned towards the back lane, "We don't want to be late now." His white hair stood out from his pinkish skull like feathers. He wore a blue terry housecoat, flannel pajamas, and broken-down leather slippers. He looked like a skinny wizard, searching his pockets for magic potions. He walked toward the white clapboard garage, turned and walked back towards the house, checked the side door, locked it, and headed towards the garage again. He stood in the middle of the laneway, teetering back and forth on his heels and toes, hesitating.

The bus pulled up and the door wheezed open.

Jess waved at the driver. She picked up her bag. "Go back in the house, Ernie."

"Oh, there you are, Yvonne. Time for school."

"I'm Jess. I'm your neighbour."

"Is that your bus?" Ernie stood in the laneway, the belt on his terry robe slipping. He looked puzzled. "I'm not ready yet."

"You don't have to go, Ernie. You're retired."

The bus driver honked. Jess didn't know what to do. She couldn't very well leave Ernie standing there like a helpless child, his thin blue-veined hands reaching out to her.

Thank goodness, Ruth came from behind the house wiping her hands on her red sweatsuit top, leaving traces of dirt from the compost bin. She shook her head. "What are we going to do with you, Ernie Mather? I thought you were vacuuming the rugs. I suppose you've locked the door on us...."

2. On the School Bus

"Too bad about Ernie." Brian leaned across the aisle in the bus. "Imagine him asking what we were celebrating at the funeral. Poor old guy. Grandpa Ernie's gone gaga. I call him the gaga geezer." Brian dropped his mouth open, hung his tongue loose, wiggled his head and rolled his eyes.

"You are so gross, Brian. Besides, he was never your grandpa." Jess's face reddened, her voice was shrill. She craned her neck to watch as Ruth and Ernie moved toward their front door. Ruth was guiding Ernie by the elbow, nattering away at him.

The bus pulled away from the curb.

"Ernie was so my grandpa. He acted as father of the bride at my mom and dad's wedding."

"That was only because your mom nursed with Grandma Ruth. But my dad and the

Mathers' kids were buddies in junior high. Ruth helped deliver me. The Mathers are my godparents. Ruth and Ernie looked after me when I was a baby. That's why my folks bought the house next door. The Mathers needed a grandkid, because their kids didn't give them any. I'm it, not you."

"Ruth looked after me too."

"So, Ruth's been your babysitter. That's not the same. Ernie's known me all my life." Jess could feel tears gathering. Stupid Brian. He could still get to her. Why did he have to change into a smart aleck?

"Ernie used to take both of us fishing, remember." Brian's voice sounded sad.

Jess glanced over her shoulder. For a moment she stared at Brian, wishing she could talk to him, wondering if she could share with him how scared and worried she was. Her foot hit her survival kit-sportsbag, reminding her of how equipped she was for any emergency. She didn't need anyone else, especially not Brian, not the way he turned everything into a joke, even Ernie's illness.

"That was before you turned into a clown." Jess stood. "I'm going to move."

"There's no other seats, Jess," Brian whispered. "You're stuck with me."

Jess slumped in her seat and tried to ignore him. She pulled her orange socks up and rebuckled the side pockets of her sportsbag. Maybe this bag really was getting too heavy, maybe she had too much in it, like her mom said. But she needed this stuff to survive.

You never knew when bad things might happen. It was good to be prepared. But some things you couldn't prepare for, it seemed, no matter how well you packed your bag. There was a lump in her throat as big as a ping-pong ball. Great cats shouldn't die. Friends shouldn't turn into clowns. Old people shouldn't lose their memories.

Brian poked her shoulder as the bus pulled up in front of the school. "Better watch it, Jess. You're somewhere in la-la land, absent-minded as old Ernie."

Jess shuddered as the words hit her. She draped her heavy sportsbag over her right shoulder, pushed past Brian, and hurried off the bus. She dodged through the line of kids and a gaggle of primary students by the side door and headed towards the bathroom. Her sneakers went plunkety-plunkety on the polished tile floor. The purple door to the girls' washroom squeaked as she opened it.

Jess ran water over her hands and splashed some on her face. She listened to the gurgle and splash and imagined sitting quietly by the side of a river or a lake, fishing with the old Grandpa Ernie and the younger Brian. She let the warm water run over her hands until she calmed down. Jess had memories heavier than her sportsbag with its strained seams. It felt as if her insides might split from the weight.

The washroom smelled of disinfectant and years of kids hanging around. The closed-in smell made Jess feel sick to her stomach. She pushed open the door.

"Great socks," her teacher said as she passed.

Brian was drinking at the water fountain. He shook his black mop in her direction. Had he been waiting for her?

"I miss Ernie, too, you know." His face had a puzzled frown. "Are you mad at me or something? We used to be friends."

"Ernie's not dead, he's just losing his memory, Brian."

"He's got Alzheimer's disease, Jess. He'll never get better."

"Mind your own business!" Jess shouted, his words ringing in her ears. She took a deep breath. "We'll take care of him, Brian. Don't get in a pickle. Don't get your relish in a jar." She clamped her mouth shut. She sounded stupid...like stupid Brian Dille, the clown, the boy who liked teasing girls, especially her. She walked past him down the hall to their classroom.

If only she could talk to Grandpa Ernie like she used to. He'd always had time to listen to her, more time than her mom even. A wide river of loneliness swept through her mind. It was one of her recurring nightmares, dreaming of trying to swim in a fast current, sinking into breathless depths, struggling to find the surface, and waking exhausted, covered with sweat. A dark dream with storm clouds, lightning, rushing water, and clawing cold.

Jess longed for things to go back to the way they were before — back to when she and Ernie and Brian fished and played rummy and silly Wild West Games and War and talked about school stuff. Jess sighed, hitched her sportsbag higher, and marched away, her right shoulder complaining from the weight. "The old Ernie's gone, Jess." Brian called after her. "Let him go."

3. Ernie in the Morning

Ernie Mather watched as the girl got on the bus. She wasn't dressed for school, wearing old blue jeans and sloppy orange socks — so where was she going? He should go with her and keep her safe. Keep her safe.

"Come on in, Ernie," the woman in the red track suit said. She unlocked the front door and held it open for him. "There's a chill in the air. I suspect we're going to have snow. Usually have a last gasp of winter close to the twenty-fourth of May holiday. First good camping weekend of the year, and the old prairie weather kicks up a snowstorm. Remember when we were snowed in out in Landis and you had to call and tell them to get a substitute teacher? That was before you became a principal, when you were teaching grade five and six."

She knew more about his life than he did,

15

this woman. Why did she keep telling him all these little details about his past? Were they important? For her, or for him?

He must have known her a long time. Her name was Ruth, a good Biblical name. Ruth in the Bible had said, "Wherever you go, I will go." Ernie was going someplace where nobody could follow. He did not want to disappoint this old friend, though, so he followed her inside.

He went to the stove and put the kettle on and walked away.

"Turn on the burner, Ernie, there's a good guy." Ruth watched him from the kitchen chair where she was putting on her pink knitted slippers. Ernie made his way back across the kitchen. Ruth came and stood too close behind as he turned on the burner. Her slippers made no noise, but he could feel her breath on his neck. He shuddered.

He walked over and checked the locks on the back door. He pulled back the curtains to let the sun shine over the sink, glisten on the taps. It must be morning. Not time for bed. But he felt tired. Too tired for words.

Ruth was busy getting out the teacups and saucers, a comfortable clinking of china on china. So Ernie sat on one of the maple kitchen chairs, let his hand slide over the polished wooden surface. It was silky smooth and honey coloured, and solid as a rock. Ernie liked solid things. So much of his life these days was dreams and dizziness.

"We're going visiting today, Ernie. To a sunny place with flowers. You can make new friends." Ruth beamed at him. "You're in for a great treat."

"Don't want to go. Don't like treats."

"We've always liked going places, Ernie."

"What?"

Ruth repeated what she had said, louder.

"Don't shout. I'm not deaf, you know," he growled.

Ruth slapped the teacup down in front of Ernie so hard the tea spilled onto the saucer. He looked up at her, frowning, picked up his hankie and mopped the saucer.

"Oh, Ernie," Ruth said with a sigh. "You aren't easy to get along with these days."

"Was I before?"

"Yes." She sat down with her tea and stirred it silently. "Everyone said you were a good principal, tough but fair. We always liked going places, meeting new people, and seeing new things. When we were young and I was on nights in emergency at the hospital, I'd pick you up after work and we'd drive to the country or to Lake Wabamun and picnic." Ruth sighed again. "Even in winter. We'd cross-country ski, or fish."

"I like fishing. I remember that." Ernie felt a moment's pleasure. A memory of poles and bait and leaping fish bubbled up, and he grasped it like a life raft. "I fished up north, didn't I?" He rubbed his chin in an excited way, willing the memory to expand. Instead, it disappeared, and he was left feeling his bristly beard.

17

"I wish you'd remind me to shave in the mornings," he said gruffly.

Ernie wandered down the hall towards the bathroom, trailing his fingers along the wall, feeling each bump on the wallpaper, repeating over and over to himself. "I'm going to shave. I'm going to shave." Panic grew as he entered the bright little room with the maroon fuzzy mat, the maroon toilet seat cover, the maroon drinking glass. His hand caressed the seat cover as he put it down. He was a gentleman and gentlemen always put the seat down after using the toilet. His mother had taught him that. Ernie remembered the tiny little woman with brown hair rolled in a bun, the hairpins falling out as she worked. A crowded house full of hairpins. He had been a good boy and where had it all gone? He rubbed his hands on the maroon towelling, the nubby bumps touching the palms of his hands. He grinned as he shambled back down the hall in his old brown leather slippers.

The woman was sitting at the table nursing her cup of tea. She did not see him right away, because her eyes were looking inward and whatever she saw in there was very sad. Her mouth trembled.

A floorboard creaked under his left foot and the woman glanced up. The expression on her face changed so fast that Ernie could not remember what he had seen before. She smiled like his mother, but her eyes were slow to pick up the grin. She seemed far away.

"You didn't shave, Ernie. You went to

shave." Her voice rasped like a nail.

"Why are you angry? What have I done? You never tell me anything." He tried the back door, wanting to escape. "Am I a prisoner here?" he shouted.

Ernie sat down again at the maple table with the carved legs, the handmade tablecloth, and the bowl of plastic fruit. He put his head between his hands, felt the pressure of those hands on his temples and his ears, felt unwanted tears gather. It was not this woman's fault. He hated it when he lost his temper. A gentleman doesn't lose his temper, doesn't blame others, doesn't cry over his troubles. Ernie couldn't remember when he had been a gentleman last. He was afraid he would never be one again.

After a few moments Ruth wrapped her arms around him. She handed him a giant white hankie and he blew his nose.

"Why don't you go and have a nap, Ernie," she said quietly. "I shouldn't upset you by talking about trips, talking about going visiting. We won't go if you don't want to, Ernie."

She took his hand in hers — and the touch of her strong fingers sent a current of warmth all the way to Ernie's insides. "We should marry, Ruth."

"We are married, Ernie, we've been married for fifty-one years. We had a big party last year in the backyard with all our friends."

"Of course we did. I remember that." Ernie wished he did remember, wished he didn't have to lie, but he wanted this secret to remain hidden as long as possible. He had records kept somewhere to help him, but where? Some days were pretty good. This one wasn't, was it?

They walked down the hall to the bedroom together. The light peach walls, the peach comforter, lampshades, drapes, and nubby carpet beneath his feet welcomed him. He felt as if he had been up too long — for a year or two. Ruth helped him take off his robe and get under the covers. The bed was safe and solid. The dizziness subsided. He would sleep, and maybe when he woke the fog would have lifted. Stray tears ran from the corners of his eyes.

"Who are we going to visit?" he asked. His voice sounded like an old man's. His pale parchment hands on the comforter were old man's hands. Had he mislaid his life, his memories? Or had they been stolen? If he had truly lost all those years, what would he do? Human beings were designed to remember and reflect. Consciousness was the greatest gift. Better than hairpins. Why was he thinking about hairpins? That was a silly thing to think about. Ernie closed his eyes and prayed, repeating the few phrases he could still remember. Like the rug, the towel, the comforter, the prayer felt solid and soothing.

He slept curled on his side, his left arm wrapped around his body, his left hand grasping his right shoulder, hugging his bones like a lonely child in a cold and strange world.

4. Ernie Makes Plans

When Ernie woke he felt better. The fog had cleared and he knew what he had to do. This illness of his was as hard on those he loved as it was on him. It was not fair to them. He would have to take things into his own hands. But first he had to talk to God.

He got up quickly, pulled on khaki pants and a tan turtleneck, and grabbed his spring jacket and cap from the closet. He opened the bedroom door cautiously. His wife was talking on the phone.

"Yes, he's sleeping like a baby. He had a really bad spell this morning. Called for David and Yvonne as if they were still kids out playing somewhere. Thought he was still teaching school. Locked us out of the house. Panicked when I mentioned the trip. I didn't even get around to telling him it was to visit the day program for Alzheimer patients. But

21

we don't talk about that, do we?"

There was a pause as the person on the other end of the line spoke.

"I know you don't agree with me. You're a different generation. As far as I'm concerned, you tell too much. How's telling him he's got a terminal disease going to help? What he doesn't know, doesn't hurt him, Naomi."

Ernie slipped into the bathroom and ran a razor over his stubble. He wished Ruth would remind him to shave. He couldn't afford to let little things slip. Before long his whole life would be a shambles. But he and Ruth didn't talk about it. He hated the dishonesty, the pretending. He wanted company facing this. His heart squeezed in his chest as if a giant had a hold of it. Ruth's voice drifted into the room.

"I hear him in the bathroom, Naomi. I'll call you later after the visit — if he'll go, that is. He can be so stubborn."

Ernie walked into the kitchen, where shafts of sunlight held dancing motes of dust. He took Ruth in his arms and kissed her, watched the worry in her eyes begin to fade.

"I must have slept the morning away. What's for lunch?"

"Lentil soup."

"Thought I'd walk down to the church and back to clear my head."

"You won't be long?"

"I'm all right, Ruth. I just want to stretch my legs...and my spirit." He rummaged in the telephone table for his prayer book and New Testament, tucked them into his jacket pocket with the neatly folded hankie and the house keys. He bent and kissed his wife on the forehead. Ruth's eyes were still troubled. He wished he could tell her it would soon be all over. She had been a wonderful companion and wife. Her hair and bushy eyebrows were still dark, but her competent nurse's hands betrayed her age with freckles, dark veins, and thinner skin. She smelled of Ivory soap and lilac-scented shampoo. Getting older hadn't been hard on her. She was still a smart, vital person. One of the lucky ones.

"Do you need gloves?"

"For Pete's sake, I'm not a baby yet."

"I could come with you."

"You don't like church."

Ernie walked the three blocks to the small Anglican church. He let himself in the newly painted oak door, allowing his hand to rest on the cool hammered-iron door handle.

He slid into a dark mahogany pew halfway down the centre aisle. He let the warmth of the wood, the smoothness of the crimson-cushioned kneeling bench, the peaceful altar, cross, and banners, and the mellow tones from the pipe organ soothe his mind and heart. He prayed the prayers of the day, read the Gospel lesson, and sat in the stillness listening to the organist rehearse the hymns for Sunday. The long weekend was coming soon. He and those nice kids had always fished in a northern lake on the long weekends.

This illness was more than he could bear. If it was his body breaking down, he could take it more easily, but not his mind. He loved to think, to plan, to remember. Life was a gift, but did he have a life if he couldn't reflect on his life journey? Every day he felt less in touch. He couldn't stand not having control over things, not being able to remember anything or anybody. He couldn't stand seeing Ruth worried, the neighbours too — Naomi and little Jess. He shook his head. He wished God would answer his prayers, make his decisions, but God kept handing the decisions back. That's what God was like.

He sighed and thought of his favourite Hebrew Scripture — it had his middle name in it, maybe that's why he liked it so much. He would have it inscribed on his gravestone — he should write it down while he was lucid. But even as he thought of writing something down, Ernie felt the slow thrum of the fog in his head like a muffled roar of rapids in a rushing river.

He would hurry home while he still remembered the way; he'd forgotten his map. He would trust Ruth and God to keep him safe until the next time that his mind was clear enough so he could think and plan. If he had the courage he would take things into his own hands. He would walk away from it all.

Ernie Enoch Mather wrote in the front of his prayer book in shaky ballpoint pen —

"And Enoch walked with God and was not, for God took him."

5. Water-bombs

Jess straightened the row of clay models along the window ledge of the art room on the Wednesday before the May long weekend. Mom was picking her up after work, so Jess was helping the art teacher until she came.

Brian's South American peasant figure sleeping with his head resting on his knees was still damp. It was really well done. Brian was good at art, better than anyone else in the class, she had to admit that. Ernie had kept drawing pencils and markers for both of them. She had preferred the blocks, the Lego, the construction sets. Not art.

Tomorrow they would paint the pottery and take it home. Her mother would put Jess's Mexican sombrero on the shelf with all the other class projects she had brought home. If Mom ever married someone else and they bought a new house, would they take all Jess's treasures with them? She didn't like the thought of moving, much less losing track of her things. "Don't borrow tomorrow's worries," Grandpa Ernie would say. "Today has enough of its own." Jess figured that must be in the Bible somewhere. Ernie always quoted Scripture, especially from the New Testament.

She stacked a haphazard pile of first graders' pet pictures made of bits of coloured wool, felt, and glue. One of the kids had made an orange cat out of wool the colour of Jess's socks. Good old Midas. Jess blinked back tears and stared out the window. A magpie scolded a squirrel on the school lawn. Maybe it was her fault that Midas was dead. Maybe they should have kept him in, or put him on a long leash like Miss Mason who kept two white Persians on long thin red ropes in the laneway, and everyone in the neighbourhood knew enough to untangle them when they walked by. If Jess got another cat, maybe she would keep it on a line.

She had wiped the counter by the window with the damp dust rag three times while she'd been thinking. She opened one of the windows and shook the rag, watching the dust rise. She could see the Seniors Centre across the ravine from her school. It had condominiums, a nursing home and extended care facility, and a drop-in centre. They were building a new wing for Alzheimer patients. For Ernie, maybe. She sighed.

Between the school and the Seniors Centre, was a wide ravine with Whitemud Drive running at the bottom of it. There were jogging trails along the lip and a skinny wooden bridge for bicycles and walkers.

A short thin old man came walking across the bridge. He was striding like an old soldier on parade. He carried a full pitcher and a stack of white paper cups. His white hair blew in the breeze. Was he going on a picnic? Meeting friends? The jug was slopping over because he was walking so fast. Something about the jaunty way he moved made Jess lean forward and peer through the window. It was Grandpa Ernie.

He stopped in the middle of the footbridge and put the pitcher on the railing and leaned over. He took off his tan golf jacket and folded it, laid it on the wooden slats that made the bridge deck. What was he doing?

Jess flew out the door. Her footsteps echoed in the empty school corridor. She dodged one forgotten Mickey Mouse sneaker outside the kindergarten door. The front door banged behind her as she spurted down the walk, pausing briefly to check for traffic. The air was heavy with the smell of exhaust fumes from the cars in the ravine. She brushed by a brilliant yellow forsythia bush, an early purple lilac, and a prickly wild rosebush. A muscle car headed down the ramp to the throughway, the music blaring from both speakers.

Ernie was stepping up onto the bottom railing

of the bridge. He was leaning out. He had a paper cup in his hand.

"Ernie! Don't do it!" Jess screamed as she raced along the bridge, her sneakers banging the planks. She grabbed him by the waist and hauled him off the railing. The two of them engaged in a funny dance as Ernie tried to break away. His eyes were startled as a deer's. Jess clenched her jaw as she wrestled with him. He pushed her away with all his might. Neither of them spoke. He ran from her, back towards the Seniors Centre, stopped and hurled the paper cup with all his force over the edge so that it sailed through the air and down into the ravine beneath their feet, where the cars raced by at eighty kilometers an hour.

Jess shook her head in astonishment. A pitcher of water, a stack of cups, and Ernie. He wasn't trying to jump on the road. He was water-bombing cars like some stupid kid.

"Oh, Ernie," she laughed in relief. Her pounding heart slowed.

He was standing out of reach, staring at her suspiciously, his head cocked to one side like a robin with a worm. Then he tiptoed back to his jug and the stack of cups.

"I've always wanted to do this," he said. "When I was a school principal over there." He pointed behind Jess towards her school. He bent and filled another cup to the brim with water and ice cubes, stepped on the lower railing, and tossed the cup onto the roof of a big shiny black car.

"Isn't it against the law?"

"Children are so law-abiding." Ernie shrugged and tossed another cup of water. Ice cubes flew through the air with sunlight glinting on them. Water spilled like raindrops. Jess leaned over the railing and stared at the paper cups rolling around the road, amazingly intact, until a giant furniture truck smushed them.

"Here, try it, you'll like it." Ernie handed Jess an overflowing paper cup. One ice cube escaped and skittered along the wooden planks underfoot.

Jess held the cup in her hand, not knowing what to do. She sipped the water, then drank it in one gulp. Ernie meanwhile was leaning further out over the railing. He dropped two more cups. One hit the roof of a red sports car.

"Bullseye!"

"Those people in there," he pointed towards the Seniors Centre. "They play stupid games. They smile a lot. They want me to play too." He dropped another bomb. "I ran away."

Jess sighed. She stared at Ernie, trying to figure out what to do. "Maybe you and I should go home."

"I've still got three cups."

Jess nodded. In some ways Ernie hadn't changed. Once he started something, he wanted to finish it. It didn't matter if it was a game of crokinole, or gin rummy, or singing his way through the old song books in Ruth's piano bench.

A police car with its light flashing, siren wailing,

came speeding down the Whitemud and headed up the ramp. What if they arrested Grandpa Ernie for being a nuisance? Was he breaking the law? She could see the headlines now — "Runaway Grandpa Water-bombs Cars on Whitemud."

"Let's go home, Ernie."

"Do you know where I live?"

"You live next door to me."

"How convenient. What will we do with the pitcher? They'll want their pitcher back."

"I'll take it back tomorrow, Ernie."

"What a wonderful child you are. Has anyone ever told you what a wonderful child you are?"

"Yeah, you and Ruth and my mom, you're always telling me." Ever since Dad left, you've been the only family I've had, she thought, and now you're leaving me too, and it scares me. Mom has Ruth to talk to. I had Midas. Jess felt suddenly cold as ice.

They walked slowly towards the school, Jess carrying the pitcher and Ernie with his golf jacket over his arm. Jess's mother was just getting out of the green Volvo.

"Where have you two been?"

Ernie glanced at Jess and grinned like a naughty kid, put his finger to his lips.

"Walking," Jess motioned to the path, the bridge. She tossed the pile of reports and papers strewn across the back seat into a box and helped Ernie into the car.

"We have to talk," she whispered, speaking over the roof at her mom. "He was water-bombing cars. He ran away."

Ernie rolled down the window. "Don't forget to lock the school. Have to lock the school. The janitor forgets, and I'm in charge, you know."

"We'll look after it, Ernie." Naomi said. She glanced at Ernie, sighed, and pushed down the kiddie lock on the back door of the Volvo.

Jess and her mom walked into the school together so Jess could get her sportsbag.

"Ruth was taking him to visit the day class for early Alzheimer patients."

"He didn't like it."

"We better rescue Ruth."

"What are we going to do about Ernie, Mom? He's getting worse. He could have gotten lost. It scared me. I think it scared him too."

"It's hard when it's someone you love, isn't it?" Mom wrapped an arm around her shoulder and hauled the sportsbag. "You really are going to have to do something about this bag, Jess. It weighs a ton."

Naomi Baines started humming a familiar tune — something about whistling a happy tune so no one would figure out she was afraid. Ernie used to sing it to them.

"Oh, Mom, that's so corny."

"To each her own way — I sing. You carry the world on your shoulder."

Ernie was sitting quietly, with his eyes shut. He had gone to sleep. Naomi and Jess got in the front seat.

"You didn't answer my question, Mom. What

31

are we going to do about Ernie?"

"Leave Ernie to Ruth and me. We'll take care of things." Naomi drove slowly over to the Seniors Centre. "You've got school and gymnastics and being a kid. We've hidden the camper and car keys. We've put inner and outer locks on the doors. Ruth and I want to keep Ernie home as long as possible. Home is the best place for all of us — young and old. It's a big adjustment for really old people to move out of their homes, especially the fragile elderly or the ones with dementia. We're building a really nice centre for patients, but it isn't finished yet. We want to get Ernie in there. It's homey."

Sometimes her mom talked like a health care worker, not a person. "Ernie isn't a case, Mom, he's our friend." Jess protested. "You talk about him like he's a patient, talk to me like I'm on staff. I'm his little Jess, his fishing partner, remember."

"Jess, relax. Let Ruth and me handle this. You probably missed being a kid when you were eight and nine, helping me get on my feet after your dad left. I'm all right now. I'm all grown up. I want you to enjoy being a kid. I don't want you being a little adult like I had to be. Okay, honey? Leave the job of being a grownup to me." She turned right after the red light changed on the other side of the intersection by the concrete overpass.

"I want Ernie at home too. I could help. I just did, didn't I?"

Jess didn't wait for an answer. Talk about

being a grownup, would she? Jess didn't point out how her mom forgot to go to the bank and had to borrow money from her, or left the vacuum cleaner in the hall for days. She was sorry her mom's mother had been such a crabby old lady, made Naomi's childhood a real trial. Maybe that's why Ruth and Naomi had become like family. Ruth wasn't crabby. But Jess didn't know how to tell either of them how worried she was. She hated feeling like a useless kid. She hadn't been able to save Midas. At least let her help save Ernie.

Her mother had gone back to humming a song about keeping her head up even when she was afraid. She parked the car in her usual spot and, carrying the empty pitcher, disappeared into the Seniors complex. Two joggers in black-and-purple spandex shorts sprinted by. The river of cars on the Whitemud hummed. Jess sat in the car by the yellow brick Seniors Centre and looked across the ravine at the yellow brick school where she went every weekday. Both buildings had big windows in the front and ramps for wheelchairs. In her mind's eye she could still see Ernie standing on the bridge halfway between the school and the Seniors Centre. She had been afraid he was going to jump. Those tense moments were scorched on her brain like a cowboy's red-hot branding iron on a steer's flank. She would have to keep an eye on him, even if her mom and Ruth were doing the same.

"Have we been abandoned?" Ernie asked as

he awoke. "I say, have we been abandoned out here?"

Ruth and Naomi came hurrying through the front door. Mom unlocked the kiddie lock on the back seat so Ruth could sit beside Ernie. Ruth had to sit with a box of Naomi's files and papers on her lap. She tut-tutted and looked at her husband. Jess wished she could shut her ears. She knew what Ruth was going to say.

"You might have gotten lost, Ernie."

6. Flight

Friday of the May long weekend Jess stood on the porch with her sportsbag at her feet waiting for the school bus. She was looking forward to a great time. She and her mom were leaving for Banff Saturday morning. They were going to spend "quality time" together. She had promised to repack her sportsbag after school. Put in useful things like a spare sweater and a swimsuit. She could hardly wait. She tugged up her Midas socks. A shock of sadness like a bucket of cold water washed over her. She remembered something she had to do.

Jess jogged to the back yard where the rosebush on Midas's grave was struggling to survive. She grabbed an ice cream bucket from the back step and upturned it over the scrawny bush. "There, in case there's a frost or a snowstorm."

"Started talking to plants, have you, Jess?"

Ruth was backing out of the driveway that ran between the two houses. Her Ford Escort wagon was sparkling clean. Jess eyed her neighbour's usually dusty car. "Ernie was a great help yesterday. He washed the car and the camper. He's trying to talk me into going away this weekend. He followed me all over the house, talking about fishing. Wore himself and me right out."

Jess looked over at the house, trying to spot Ernie.

"He's sleeping," Ruth sighed. "Couldn't sleep last night. He kept getting up. He'd put his clothes on and try the doors. He even used some bad language when he couldn't get out, and you know how he hates swearing. I told him it wasn't morning, I showed him the moon through the window. Told him to go back to bed." Ruth clutched the steering wheel as if it was a life preserver and she was in deep water.

Jess thought she saw the drapes in the Mathers' house move, a face disappear. Her good mood had completely disappeared. In its place was a well of anxiety.

"Do you want a ride to school?"

"No thanks, I'll wait for the bus."

Grandma Ruth drove off. Jess walked up the laneway towards the street. Brian Dille spotted her, waved frantically, and started doing back flips on his lawn. Showoff! What a clown! She was so mad at him, trying to tell her how to run her life, telling her to forget

Ernie. As if he'd been such a great friend lately.

All year he'd been hanging out with those bullies, giggling, chasing Jess and some of the smaller girls. One of the times that had made her really mad was last fall. The scene stuck out in her mind. The amazing blue sky, the dusty schoolyard, the forbidden puddles that the little kids got into, the smell of crabapples, the class in their outfits for games outdoors, and her old friend Brian Dille — he'd stood with "the boys" laughing at the girls and the way they threw the ball, making smart remarks as they chose teams for volleyball. He'd shouted from the side lines, "We'll take Tara as a spare-a, but Jess is a mess." What a clown, what a dummy, what a bummer. She certainly didn't miss him. No way. Let him stew in his own juice. It was no skin off her nose if he wanted to be a nincompoop, as Ernie called all stupid drivers.

The back door of the Mather house flew open. Ernie emerged, carrying a battered suitcase and his fishing gear. He peered around the corner of the house, scanned the back yard, and tiptoed to the truck camper with an orange tarp over it that was parked next to the garage. He pushed his Northern Alberta Dairy Pool cap away from his forehead. That was Ernie's prized fishing hat. Jess and Brian both had matching caps — only smaller. Hers was probably too small now.

"Ernie, where are you going?"

He looked back towards his house and put his finger to his lips. "It's a secret." He started

37

pulling the tarp off the camper and folding it.

Jess ran to help. Ernie had some plan in mind. He had the truck keys in his hand and he was unlocking the cab door. Where'd he get them? Whatever he was up to was going to mean trouble, worse trouble than water-bombing cars. Jess's mind went a mile a minute.

"Ernie, could you drop me at school?"

"I'm retired now. Don't go to school any more."

Ernie had a sly look on his face. He was acting like a sneaky kid.

"Ruth wants to go, doesn't she? Shouldn't you wait for her?" A shiver went down Jess's back.

Ernie shook his head, opened the back door of the camper, and tossed in his suitcase and fishing gear. The stuff landed with a thud. "She doesn't like fishing. She likes visiting relatives, sitting in chairs, balancing teacups. I like being outdoors."

Jess heard rather than saw the school bus pull away. She had been standing in the shadow of the Mather garage, so the bus driver couldn't see her. Fine group of friends she had. It was a cinch Brian wouldn't care, not about her, not about Ernie, the gaga geezer, as he'd nicknamed him when he'd brought Ernie home from the West Edmonton Mall. Ernie had been feeding scraps of paper to the goldfish in one of the fountains.

Ernie climbed into the cab of the old blue truck, whistling one of his Second World War songs. He sounded really cheerful.

"You aren't supposed to be driving, Ernie," Jess scolded. "Where'd you get the keys? What if you run out of gas?"

"Now, don't you worry your beautiful little head, sweetheart. I talked the missus into filling the tank yesterday. I'm on a roll, little lady. There's no stopping me now." He was doing his John Wayne tough-guy impersonation. He had old Western movies on video, and she and Brian had watched them over and over. His eyes looked steely and his jaw firm.

Jess looked longingly at the street, willing someone they knew to drive by. She glanced over at her house, wishing she had time to phone her mom.

She tried one more time — "Ernie, I missed my bus. You have to take me to school."

"No, I don't. Don't go to school any more. I'm retired." He repeated what he had said a minute ago and chuckled as if it was a great joke. He started the motor, looked in the rearview mirror, and prepared to back up.

Jess's mind whirred like a helicopter. Someone had to stop Ernie from running away like this. He might get lost. He might have an accident. But her mom had said it wasn't Jess's problem.

Jess made a quick decision, heart beating like a speeded-up metronome, palms sweating. She grabbed her heavy old sportsbag, ran around the front of the truck, yanked open the door, and leapt in. She did up her seat belt.

"I don't want company," Ernie shouted. "I want to be alone."

Jess felt the slap of his words on her face. This was not Grandpa Ernie talking. Ernie Mather loved her, always had. He liked being with her. She and Brian were his sergeants and he was Lieutenant Mather of the Princess Pats. She glanced over at the wiry, determined old man ignoring her, driving the truck down the street as if his life depended on it. She was alone in a beat-up old camper truck with a stranger.

Ernie sped along the Whitemud until he came to 111th. He turned north. He had one eye on the speedometer and the other on the road. He whistled another song. Jess wondered if she sang along whether he'd snap out of this frantic mood, whether she'd be able to get him to stop.

" 'Keep the home fires burning....' "

Jess put her hand on Ernie's arm. "I want to go home, Ernie."

"Now, sergeant, you know we can't leave until after the next patrol. We've got a hill to take. Bert, you and I will soldier on until the end."

All their games came back to her. It made Jess feel very old. She and Brian and Ernie had played Sesame Street — with Ernie being Ernie, Jess being Bert, and Brian being Big Bird because he had a yellow T-shirt. They had played war and they had played rootin-tootin Westerns. They played on road trips, fishing trips, or between crokinole and parcheesi games.

Jess watched as Ernie guided the truck past

the university and across the river on the Groat bridge. Traffic streamed by. The sun shone brightly, heating up the side window and her right arm, but Jess felt cold inside.

"We're not playing games here, Ernie. This is for real. Let me out at the doughnut shop on 111th."

Ernie frowned. He studied her with a slantwise look. "You'll tell." The truck rolled on. The old motor hummed a doleful tune.

Jess shivered. Her muscles tensed so tight she was quaking. The truck cab felt hot, as if it was shrinking around her. Her stomach was queasy. Beads of sweat formed on her forehead. She could not remember ever being this frightened.

"You're sick, Ernie. You need help," Jess started to cry. She fished in the glove compartment for tissues. Good-hearted, sensible Ruth always kept Kleenex there. She buried her face in a tissue. Everything was upside down. "You can't run away, Ernie. Remember, you wouldn't let me run away when I was a little kid. You said I needed to stay home until I was old enough to manage on my own. You said no one should leave home without a good plan."

Ernie wasn't talking. Jess stared out the window, watching the flowering plum and crab on the banks along Groat Road. She remembered as if it were yesterday her six-year-old self with her pale blue doll suitcase, filled with underwear and socks and a pocket teddy bear, marching

41

down the sidewalk the day after her dad had left for good. Ernie had caught up with her at the corner of 148th Street and the park. He had taken her hand and walked her back home. That's when they had become good buddies. That's when all the games had started in earnest. Brian had joined in the fun because Ruth looked after him when his mom was working evenings.

"I have a plan." Ernie spoke so low Jess wasn't sure if she had heard right.. Her brain felt squeezed. Something about his voice, the sadness in his eyes despite the games, something about an old man who loved company heading off by himself, made her very nervous.

Ernie slowed the truck, putting on the turn signal. Jess made another decision. The back of her neck tingled as she picked one of her familiar old roles.

"Well, Lieutenant, maybe you're right. I wouldn't want to go AWOL before the next patrol. What kind of a sergeant would I be if I did that?"

"Absent With Out Leave, oh my, no."

"So we'll go together, right?"

"I could go ahead and scout the lay of the land," Ernie parried. "Check for snipers."

"No soldier should go alone. Remember our motto."

"Is that our motto?"

"One of them." Jess heaved a sigh of relief. Ernie had moved back into the line of traffic heading past Westmount and onto St. Albert

Trail to the north. Other trailers and campers getting an early start were going the same way.

"Some varmint hid the truck keys in the freezer, little lady." Ernie pulled his tractor cap down over his eyes. "But I found them." He started whistling the old cowboy song, "Don't Fence Me In."

Except for the frightened look in his eyes, Jess could have imagined they were going on a planned fishing trip back when she was eight or nine. But she missed Brian. He was the deputy in this movie, and he might be able to figure out how to get Sheriff Mather off his horse.

As they travelled through St. Albert, Jess tried one more time.

"What about callin' the wimmen folk so they won't get to worryin'?" she said in her best Western accent. "Or stop for some grub?"

"Where I'm goin' they don't need to know. Where I'm goin' no one needs grub." Ernie pushed the accelerator to the floor and gripped the steering wheel in both hands.

Jess made a grab for the dashboard. The truck rattled and banged its way along Highway Two heading north. A flock of ducks rose from a slough. At her feet her heavy sportsbag slumped onto her left foot. She tugged up her Midas socks and prayed that she had everything with her she would need to survive the journey ahead. Talk about being prepared for surprises — this was a doozey!

A grey minivan loaded with camping gear

honked as it passed. The driver shook his fist out the window. Ernie veered to the right. He'd been taking up too much of the road.

"Tarnation, those city slickers, in such an all-fired hurry to escape. Don't they know there ain't no escape?"

Jess hunched her shoulders, chewed bubblegum, and felt a lippy remark coming on. She couldn't help herself.

"Then why are you running away, Ernie?"

7. Brian, the Deputy

Brian climbed on the bus, rolled his eyes up into his head to make the guys at the back laugh. But he didn't say anything funny.

"Slow today, Brian." The bus driver chided.

"What's the fuss, just drive the bus." Brian played to the kids in the seats around him, ambled down the aisle and found a seat by the window. He had to shoo a first grader out of his way. He unzipped his Edmonton Oilers jacket and turned to watch out the window for Jess. He wanted to talk to her. It bugged him that she was acting so cool, like he was a slug and she was in charge of the universe.

"So, Brian, tell us a funny story," one kid said.

Brian ignored him.

The bus pulled away from the curb in front of Jess's house with a blast of fumes. "You kids, you think I've got all day to wait," the driver ranted. "Jess Baines is just going to have to suffer. She'll have to walk. I can't be responsible for every stupid latecomer."

Brian stared through the windowpane, craning his neck to look back. Where was Jess? He'd seen her on the lane, but she must have forgotten something. It worried him. Girls have to be careful, walking to school alone. Bad things can happen.

He drummed his fingers on his math book and turned towards the window to avoid the eyes of the other kids. Something didn't feel right. There was nothing funny about this. Where was Jess?

He had watched Jess Baines walking down her laneway towards the street a few minutes ago. Ruth Mather had driven by in her car. Brian had waved at her.

Ernie hadn't been with her.

He had wanted to wave at Jess, but instead he had started doing back flips on the lawn. Trust him to show off! But she hadn't even noticed him. Instead the loose change had fallen out of his pocket, including his seven lucky pesos from Mexico that his mom, Marie, had brought back from her last vacation with her best friends, Lucille and Linda.

Brian had scrabbled in the lawn for the two loonies and the special coins. Just as he dusted off his pants, he had spotted the last coin hidden under a dead poplar leaf. He put them all in the little leather pouch he had found in his dad's junk in the basement. Brian loved the feel of the old pigskin leather with its pinholes. He loved the way the drawstring worked. It had two tiny brass balls on the ends of the strip of thin leather that kept the pouch closed. Secretly Brian called it his "poke." Didn't gold miners have "pokes" that they kept gold dust in?

When he got to school he hung out with the boys by the back fence. They tossed pennies against a loose fence board. He kept watching for a sign of Jess.

"What's with you, Brine, you're nervous as a cat," one of the kids asked. "No jokes today?" Stupid nickname. When would they stop using it. Just because he liked pickles in his lunch. Was that a crime?

His mind raced from one thing to another. Dead cats and doing back flips and when did he become the class clown and why did people expect him to be funny even when life wasn't? He knew how to be serious.

After all, he'd been the one that found Ernie feeding the fish in the fountain at the giant mall and taken him back home. Ernie had been tearing up bits of paper napkin and tossing them in the tank, watching them float, get wet, and sink. Float, get wet, and sink. Brian could still remember the tight feeling in his throat as he'd watched Ernie, as he'd talked him into going home, as he'd looked in Grandpa Ernie's once clear eyes and seen a stranger. He remembered shutting the door to Ernie's house after Ruth had welcomed Ernie home and thanked Brian. With the snap of the lock he had closed more than a door. He'd felt really torn up inside, just like those scraps of paper sinking in the pond. But a guy has to move on, doesn't he?

He pushed his hand through his tangled mass of tight black curls and walked into the school. He checked the hooks to see if Jess's jacket was there. He checked by the girl's washroom. He looked in the library and the office.

"Something wrong, Brian?" the art teacher asked as he peered in her door.

He shrugged and went on down the hall. The bell rang. Several of the kids were missing. Their folks had gotten a head start on the weekend.

Mrs. Slater came in the door. She started with a math quiz, so Brian took the sheet and whizzed through it. Every few seconds he'd lift his head and check the door to see if Jess had arrived. He finished the quiz and put it on the corner of Mrs. Slater's desk and cruised slowly past the door, peering through the glass.

"Are you looking for someone," Mrs. Slater asked, "or just admiring the view, Brian?" She was used to his jokes.

Brian didn't feel like saying anything funny. He was worried. Couldn't a guy be worried?

"I wondered if Jess was coming. She missed the bus."

"Oooh, Jessie, where are you, Brine wants you," one of the boys hissed under his breath.

"Maybe she's gone already," Mrs. Slater said. "She's going to Banff."

"She was standing on the laneway with her sportsbag three minutes before the bus arrived."

"Mrs. Slater, the bus driver was mad at her for taking so long," one of the girls said. "Brian was too busy doing flips and rolling in the grass to notice anything."

"I'm sure there's a perfectly logical explanation, Brian. Go back to your seat."

The room went silent except for the scratching of pencils on paper. The next fastest students put their papers on Mrs. Slater's desk.

Brian was sharpening his pencil over by the windows, staring at the street, praying for Naomi's or Ruth's car to show up. It wouldn't be the first time a kid had been kidnapped in Edmonton. He knew he was an awfulizer, his dad told him he always thought of the worst possibilities first.

"Brian, will you kindly sit down? You're making me nervous," Mrs. Slater sighed.

Brian shoved his pencil in his pocket, felt the leather pouch with the seven coins in it. "I'd feel a lot better if I called my dad. He's got a new car phone and could check up on Jess."

"Oh, all right, Brian, if it will allow us to get on with life."

Brian ran down the hall to the office and picked up the phone, dialed his dad's office number, let it ring until the secretary answered. "Your dad is visiting a client in the west end.

Should I have him call you?"

"I don't know."

"Just a minute, Brian, your dad is on the other line," she said.

Brian told his dad the whole story.

"Look, I'll check with Ruth and Naomi," he said. "You go back to class."

"What if she's gone?"

"Brian, how many times do I have to tell you...."

"Don't awfulize. I know." Brian sighed. "It's just, she was right there on the curb and then she wasn't."

"Go back to class." His dad hung up.

Thirty minutes later the intercom fluttered and wheezed. "Would Brian Dille come to the office."

Brian loped down the hall. His dad was standing in the vestibule, nattering away, his mahogany face beaded with sweat. "Ernie must have found the truck keys. The truck is gone. Ernie's gone. Jess is gone. Naomi is frantic."

"Let's get out of here."

"Brian, it's not our business." His dad stood stock still in his expensive sage suit, silk shirt, silk tie. His black shoes shone.

"I bet he's gone fishing if he's taken the camper." Brian bounced up and down on his sneakers. "I wish I'd been there. Jess and I used to go."

Sonny Dille ran his hands in and out of his pants pockets a couple of times.

"Dad, we should go by the house, at least. See if there's anything we can do. Ruth might need us," Brian pleaded.

Time stood still in the vestibule of Whitemud School while Sonny Dille decided what to do. It was as if father and son were linked telepathically. By the time the minute hand on the hall clock pinged, Brian had raced for his jacket while his dad spoke to the principal, and then the two of them were running down the sidewalk to the jeep.

"The biggest question is — which way did they go?"

8. Where Are We Going?

At the new light at the T-junction in Landis, Ernie brought the camper to a grinding halt. A lumber truck barrelled through, heading towards the pulp mill. A high ridge of clouds blocked the sun, giving the dusty main street of the small town, built on the bank of the mighty Athabasca, a desolate look. Late Friday morning of the long weekend and traffic moved slowly — pickups, half-tons, loungers outside of the Landis Hotel and Bar. Two women with babies in strollers came out of the IDA drugstore.

"Ernie, I need sunscreen." Jess tried once more to get to a phone. By now her mom would be frantic. Ruth would have called Naomi. One of them would have checked the school. "You don't want me suffering from the harmful rays of the sun." She was using her best damsel-in-distress voice. Only it wasn't fake. She was scared. Maybe she had made the wrong decision. She clenched her teeth, turned a plaintive, begging face towards Ernie.

Ernie ignored her and scratched the stubble on his chin. The light turned green. The camper behind honked.

"Which way?" he asked.

"If we're going to Baptiste Lake, we go left. If we're going to Calling Lake, we turn right." Jess shook her head. This wasn't any Hansel and Gretel story. She couldn't leave any breadcrumbs to mark the path. Wait a minute! Maybe she could. She bent down and took off one of her Midas socks and stuffed it in her jacket pocket.

Ernie turned right and parked the truck beside the road. He was clutching the steering wheel and shouting. "I can't even remember which is left and which is right. I had a plan. I had a plan." He took his left hand off the wheel, scrabbled in his pocket as if he was searching for something, and when he couldn't find anything he banged his fist on the dashboard. "I won't go to that place. I won't spend my days with strangers. Ruth shouldn't ask me."

Jess Baines was tired, thirsty, and she had to go to the bathroom. Ernie must have been really upset by that visit to the Seniors Centre. Meanwhile Jess's brain felt like it was in the middle of a tough exam and nobody knew the right answers.

She had a choice again. She could dash from the truck and call Ruth's house and risk Ernie driving away — but there was something about the steely light in his eyes when he wasn't foggy that made Jess extra worried — or she could let things ride, go with him, hope she could.... What was she hoping for? That she could bring him home safe and sound? That was impossible. Ernie would never be sound again. Jess wanted to cry. An ache filled her chest. She couldn't do this. She was a kid. Kids didn't have to make choices like this. Adults did. But Ernie wasn't an adult any more. He'd forgotten how to be an adult and Jess didn't know how yet.

She put her hand on the door handle. As they sat in the truck, Ernie had been singing and tapping the dashboard rhythmically. " 'When you walk through a storm,' " he sang, " 'hold your head up high, and don't be afraid of the dark. At the end of the storm is a golden sky and the sweet silver song of a lark.' If Ruth was here, she'd sing along. It's all about being brave and it's got larks in it. What a good song for a trip like this! I remember where I'm going. I'm going back to where I started."

He put the truck in gear. Jess took her hand off the door handle. She remembered the words to this schmaltzy old song. Her mother had been singing it the other day. It ended with the words Ernie was now singing in his thin baritone voice, all about never walking alone. She had to go with Ernie. If she didn't he'd be out in the wilderness alone. There was no telling what kind of trouble he'd get into.

They pulled into traffic and headed out of town on the road north towards Calling Lake. Jess rolled her window down and waited. On the far side of the wooden bridge over the Athabasca River, near the Landis Golf Club, a stand of diamond willow grew close to the road.

"Look, Ernie, a flock of geese," Jess pointed towards the sand and gravel company on the left side of the road. Ernie glanced that way. Meanwhile she tossed her Midas sock with all her might. It caught on one of the limbs of the diamond willow. It hung crooked, like a peculiar woolly surveyor's tag. But anyone who knew her would spot it and know which way they had gone. If anyone figured out they were up here.

Ernie was still humming. "You shouldn't have come," he said. A pickup truck passed, blowing its horn. Ernie had been driving too close to the middle of the road again. Jess was jittery just watching him manoeuvre the truck.

"Don't say that. It's not nice." Jess wanted to hit Ernie — this Ernie — not her old friend. He was like a mouthy kid. She chewed her lip and tried to calm down.

She studied her hands clasped in her lap. It was nearly noon. If she'd gone to school, she would have been at gym club. Doing a gymnastics routine was so straightforward. You practised your approach, rehearsed your moves in your head and for real, and worked really hard at your dismount. You did what the coach said. Jess rubbed her hands together, wishing she was with her teammates and there was chalk on her hands and a set of uneven bars. Instead here she was with Ernie, heading into the northern bush.

They sailed past the deserted rodeo grounds, a shed with two shiny brown horses and a black colt, and a white-and-blue house the size of a garage, attached to a trailer. Early bright geraniums waved in the breeze in a painted white tire planter on the lawn. A huge brown farm dog barked.

Ernie slowed the truck and peered off to the left. Another van roared by. "I think it's down here, little lady. We'll have to take the horses slowly from here on. Might be rustlers and other mean critters."

"The lake's not here, Ernie."

"I know that, gal."

"Ernie, if you'd tell me where we're going, maybe I could help."

"You aren't playing the game, Yvonne. What about the game?"

"I'm Jess," she whispered. Oh, how she longed for the old Ernie, the one who knew her, the one who loved her.

They had just passed a new small sawmill and lumberyard when Ernie put his foot on the brake, nearly tossing both of them through the windshield. Jess's seat belt dug into her neck as it flung her back against the seat. Ernie pulled onto a gravel road to the left, with the tv and radio tower flashing on and off, on and off. They were heading towards the Athabasca River.

Rocks spat at the windshield as a gravel truck roared past. Dust coated the truck and Jess coughed, held onto the dashboard.

"I wish you hadn't come. It complicates things." Ernie didn't look at Jess, he just stared through the window and drove. He had stopped playing cowboy.

The more Ernie said he wished she hadn't come, the more Jess was clear it was a good thing she had. Her chest felt as if a weight was pressed on it, a heavy, immovable weight.

"Maybe we should go home." She kept the anger, the fear, out of her voice.

"I'm going home," Ernie said. They passed a tiny cemetery overgrown with wild rosebushes and clover. A big wooden cross with peeling white paint tilted to the right.

"It's a wonder the Olnichuks don't fix that. I should talk to them. They're good people, related to my wife Ruth. Too bad the boy died, the one who drowned in the dugout. He was in grade six, you know. Nice boy, hard-working. I don't remember his name."

"It was a long time ago, Ernie." Jess patted his trembling hand. Maybe if she touched his hand he would remember who she was. She wanted him to remember her. Please, Ernie, come back.

"Was it? Was it long ago?" he looked really hard at her. "Weren't you in my class?"

"No, Ernie, I'm Jess. I live next door to you in

the city." In her ears her voice sounded shrill, like her mother's when she was upset.

"Of course you do. Your dad was my son's best friend. Your dad and my son went away. Are they dead, like the Olnichuk boy?"

"No, they aren't dead. My dad lives in Ontario. Your son David works in Rome. He's a famous fish scientist." Jess bit her lip, keeping the frustration out of her words.

"I know that. Might as well be dead, all of them. I probably wouldn't know them if I saw them."

Jess blinked as the truck went over a ridge in the gravel road left by the grader. "That must be hard."

"There's another boy, a dark boy with fuzzy hair and a big grin. He's good at math and drawing. Is he dead, too?"

"That's Brian Dille. He's alive. He used to come with us. He used to be our friend." Jess gripped her knees as Ernie steered back and forth over the ridge on the road. "He calls you names," Jess whispered. "I don't call you names. I won't leave you."

"Aren't friends forever?"

"Not Brian. He's a clown. He's a nincompoop."

"Children are so unforgiving."

"He laughs at the way I throw a ball. He laughs at you."

"That's not very friendly." Ernie peered through the windows, looking for something. "The Olnichuk boy was pale as moonlight when they brought him out of the water. He looked like he was sleeping peacefully. It's all a jumble in my head, you know."

"Where are we going, Ernie?" Jess's jaw hurt from keeping her teeth from chattering. "Ruth and my mom are going to worry."

"Keep your eye on the tower," Ernie said, ignoring her. "As long as we can spot the tower, we aren't far from the river or the school. My first school. It's where I started out." The old man sighed and smiled slightly. The first smile Jess had seen in weeks.

The road turned sharply to the right and then to the left. "I don't see it yet." There was a pause as Ernie slowed the truck down and peered through the windscreen. "Have they pulled it down? Watch for a little spruce tree. I planted it in front of the school. It was lonely at night after the children had gone home, but I loved it. The silence, the sound of the rushing water. I used to walk to the river after I had finished teaching the kids on a warm June day. A river is a wonderful thing. It reminds us that life is a flow, it races ahead of us. Sitting beside it all the stress of teaching would drain away. I'd fish, catch my dinner. I made $800 the second year, lived in the teacherage. Life is a circle game, a carousel, and I can't find where I got on or where to get off."

"How did you get to town, Ernie? Did you have a car, one of those funny old cars you see in movies?"

"Sometimes I had a car. Sometimes I went by river and Ruth would drive me home, my canoe tossed in the back of her dad's pickup.

It's much shorter by river."

"Wasn't it dangerous, alone on the Athabasca in a canoe?" Jess shuddered, thinking about the ancient river running by the steep wild banks she had spotted as the camper crossed the bridge. "Rivers scare me. I have nightmares."

"I thought the young liked a little danger in their lives."

"That's what you think. I don't like danger, Ernie. I don't like it at all."

"So why did you come then?" He gave her a withering glance.

Jess kept the tears from falling by staring out the window. She wished Ernie couldn't hurt her by saying mean things, by looking at her in cruel ways. It was hard to remember that he wasn't himself. Where had nice, friendly Grandpa Ernie gone?

The truck crawled along the road at a snail's pace. Jess sighed and joined Ernie in his search for the old schoolhouse. Maybe all he wanted was to drive out here and see where he had started teaching. Maybe he would be all right. Seeing the familiar landscape had calmed him down. She liked it when he talked about what life was like a long time ago. She missed that part of him so much. It made her want to cry, listening to him now, wondering how many more good conversations they would have.

"This would be a good place to die." Ernie sighed.

Each word landed like a hammer blow on Jess's heart.

9. The Old School

"Wait! Ernie, look through the trees," Jess tugged his arm. He jammed his foot on the brake. She could see a broken-down log building with a wall of small-paned windows, hidden behind a screen of spindly young poplars and a big spruce. The black shingled roof sagged. One corner of the blackened log wall had crumbled. Several windows were broken, and jagged fragments of glass reflected scant light. Moss covered the lower logs.

" 'Let me live in my house by the side of the road and be a friend to man,' " Ernie recited as he clambered over a sagging fence and strode through the waist-high bushes that overgrew the track to the school. Jess followed at a distance. He stopped and stared at a large spruce tree just to the right of the door to the schoolhouse. "That

61

can't be the small tree I planted."

The old man's eyes had taken on a wild, worried look. Jess wanted to tell him it was all right. But was it?

Ernie ran his hand along the door frame, pushed open the wood slatted door. It squeaked. His eyes, when he looked back at her, had grown large and dark. The school smelled of mildew and rotting wood. Two ancient desks leaned against the wall, their inkwells dark and empty black holes. The dusty blackboard had a hole the size of a fist. There was no chalk. A rusted potbellied stove sat in the corner and neat rows of dried mushrooms filled the closet. Some chipmunk or squirrel family had forgotten where they had stored their winter food supply.

Jess wanted to ask questions, but something blocked her throat, wouldn't let her speak. Would he answer or glare at her? In the silence the building seemed to breathe. Jess wanted to ask — When did you close? How many kids studied here? What was Ernie like when he was young?

"The piano was over in the corner. I taught the kids to sing songs. Life without singing is pretty dull and has no soul. Life without games and stories isn't worth living. Life is about imagination, memory, and love. Now I can't remember the stories, I'm forgetting the songs, and I don't recognize the people I love."

Ernie turned on his heel and stumbled out of the school, picked up a pine cone from the base of the large tree, and hurried through the trampled bushes to the truck. He started the engine.

"Don't you want to see the teacherage?" Jess hollered, running to catch up. "How long did you live here? Did Ruth live here with you?" She stood between the caragana hedge and the truck, bent down, took off her second Midas stocking and draped it over a deadfall birch by her foot.

The old man's face was red, his eyes wild. He pointed through the trees to the smaller log building. "In my mind it's so fresh and bright. It's dying. I've seen enough. Have to get out of here."

Jess clambered into the passenger's seat and buckled up quickly.

Ernie jabbed his foot on the accelerator and sped down the road. "I can't bear the thought of going into that place that woman wants me to visit."

"That woman is your wife, Ernie. And it's a nice place."

" I can't go back there. It frightens me." The old man turned and looked at Jess. For a split second she saw the old Ernie staring out at her. "Don't you see, Jess. I might wander away for good. I might never return. I can't come back here either. I'm caught between my past and my future, and no one can help me." He threw the crumpled pine cone out the window.

"Hang on!" he shouted. The motor roared. Billows of dust rose.

"Oh, Ernie!" Tears gathered in Jess's eyes,

spilling over, running down her cheeks like small rivers. She felt Ernie's pain as if it was her own, and it was black and angry and had no bottom. But she couldn't stay there long. It was too dangerous.

He was driving too fast. She wished she could remember how her mom handled people. Naomi would know what to say. Jess gripped the dashboard so tightly her knuckles whitened.

The dense pine and poplar woods crowded too close to the road. The last signs of civilization disappeared. There weren't even fenceposts or Rural Crime Watch signs. Deer tracks cut through the thick grasses and stunted willow. The sky darkened. A raven screamed. A flock of chickadees whirred across the road too close for comfort. Jess shut her eyes, afraid one of them would smash and die against the window.

An overgrown cutline, where all the trees and brush had been cleared for gas or oil exploration, crossed at an angle. Tracks from all-terrain vehicles had flattened the early spring growth. Maybe they weren't alone out here after all.

Ernie swerved the truck to miss two blackbirds feasting on a small bloody corpse. He made a sharp turn, leaving the gravel road, and turned towards the river far below. The truck banged and jangled down a rutted track towards a high, steep bank above the Athabasca. The track turned from sand to slippery wet clay. The truck threatened to bog down. The motor roared as Ernie pushed the pedal to the floor. The sharp smell of exhaust came through the open window.

Jess clutched the vinyl seat. She cringed as low branches of trees and whole bushes struck the windshield, scraping the sides of the truck and camper, as rocks and deadfall bumped and banged the bottom.

"Stop, Ernie, you'll kill us both!" she screamed. Ernie stared at her. Slowly, his eyes focused. It was like watching a light go on in a dark room.

"Oh, no!" he shouted. "What am I doing?"

Ernie slammed the brakes on. But it was too late. Ahead of them, Jess saw open sky behind the last trees before the river bank plunged down towards the water. The tires slipped in the gumbo by the ridge, the truck sliding sideways on the slick clay. It reached the edge, pitched over, rolled on its side. The camper broke free, tumbling away like a broken doll's house. The truck, released from its heavy burden, crashed through the trees and brush down, down, towards the rushing river.

Young trees on the slope snapped off, small branches broke. The truck body whined and groaned. The air filled with strident clanking noises.

Jess hugged herself tight, dug her fingernails into the fleshy upper arms as the truck flipped and righted itself again. There, they were travelling upright again, but at a dangerous tilt. She was wrenched forward, held only by her seat belt. They were going to roll, she knew it!

Suddenly, there was a huge bang. The impact reverberated to her toes. The truck came to a sudden halt. The motor died. The air stilled. The noise faded away.

Through Ernie's side window, the glass smashed into the shape of a giant spider's web, Jess could see the giant elm tree that had stopped them from tumbling all the way down to the river. Ernie's head leaned against the window. His eyes were closed, his face chalky, his hands loose in his lap. Blood spattered his shirt. Jess reached out her left hand timidly — noticed how it was shaking, noticed how pale she was, how chilled — and touched his veined right hand. It had fallen from the gear shift and hung by his side.

Bright flashes of red and black ricocheted in her skull. She could trace the blood as it ran through her veins to her heart. She had a river rushing inside her, rushing to feed her brain, her heart. She was alive. Her heart pounded like a woodpecker hammering a tree. She stared at Ernie. Fear knotted her stomach, her hands trembled. Ernie's skin was parchment soft, and warm. Anxiously she tugged at his hand.

"Ernie, wake up! Please."

She spotted a flutter of pulse in his neck. She gasped as if she'd been running a race and forced her eyes to study Ernie's body. His back trembled and the cord in his neck throbbed. She could see no more blood, but his left foot and ankle were jammed under the brake pedal on the floor of the truck and his head must be hurt where it was leaning against the window.

Slowly but carefully, she undid her seat belt and moved each limb gingerly. Except for bloody gouges in her left palm where her fingernails had dug in, a cut on her chin, a scraped knee leaking blood onto her jeans, and a lot of aches and pains, she was all right. She took three deep breaths in a row. She pushed on the truck door but it wouldn't budge. The handle was jammed. It wouldn't turn, not even an inch. The window was halfway down. She struggled with the knob and slowly rolled the window the rest of the way, the glass moaning in its track. She crawled out and dropped to the ground. Her knees buckled and she collapsed. Damp air assailed her nostrils and made her sneeze. It was laden with the smell of blossoms, disturbed earth and plants, and the foreign odours of gas, oil, metal, and exhaust. The smell of leaking gas made her stomach lurch.

The birds, stilled by the truck's thundering arrival, regained their courage. They sang lustily, scolding Jess. A small animal scurried through the brush.

Jess pulled herself up, gripping the bumper and then the hood of the truck. The overheated engine made the metal hot to touch. She moved her hand to a birch broken by the truck in passing. Its smooth bark was softer than skin. She leaned her whole body against the poor half-tree. She began to shake uncontrollably, her skin clammy, cold and hot at the same time. Her teeth chattered. Her head throbbed. Jess slipped down and leaned her back against the tree trunk. Shudders and shakes flooded over her. At least she was alive. And Ernie, he'd wake up. He must have hit his head. She wished her mother was here. She wished Grandma Ruth was here. She was a nurse, she'd know what to do.

Jess hugged her knees tightly, trying to stop the shaking, the sick feeling, the dizziness in her head.

Don't hurry, she told herself. First, collect your wits. Get your survival kit out and patch yourself up — the cuts were stinging and the blood soaking her jeans made her stomach feel squeamish. Get Ernie out of the truck and make him as comfortable as possible. Then go for help.

But ever since they'd left the old school there'd been nothing but bush. She tried to get her mind to concentrate, but part of it seemed to be shaking like her hands. Was this shock? The St. John's Ambulance lady had told them at school about shock.

Clawing the damp scarred earth, Jess pulled herself upright. Her calves hurt as if she'd pedaled her bike uphill for hours. Everything around her was extra sharp and clear as if she had been given double sight, smell, and hearing. Everything she did seemed to be in slow motion. Under her feet the leaves and moss were slippery and smelled musty like Ruth's compost bin. One hundred shades of green surrounded her. She slid down the bank to a small clearing where a deer had slept recently, the long grass trampled in a circle and crushed. Tiny white flowers sprinkled the area like stars. She glanced up towards the truck crushed against the elm, its front bumper wrapped around a green poplar, the debris from the broken camper littering the wooded slope between her and the truck. Here would be a good place to set up camp for Ernie.

Ernie's head raised. He was blinking. Jess scrambled up the rise and tried to wrench open the door on his side. It was jammed shut, blocked by the elm.

"You'll have to crawl out my side, Ernie."

"Eh?"

Jess made her way around the front of the truck to the passenger side and reached her hand through the open window. "Come on, Ernie, you can't stay in there."

The old man rubbed the left side of his head where a goose egg was forming. "I seem to be having trouble, princess."

It took several minutes for Jess to tug Ernie from behind the wheel, free his foot from between the pedals on the floor. His body didn't want to cooperate. It was stiff and wiry, didn't want to bend. His skin smelled of blood, stale sweat, and fear. His once neat polyester trousers were all greasy. When she did get him through the window, he collapsed beside the truck. His left ankle wouldn't work and his left arm hung at his side.

"Might be fire." Ernie's eyes opened wide with

fright. "Spilled gas." He tried to crawl away from the truck, but his body wouldn't work.

Jess smelled the fumes. Thank goodness Ernie was conscious and thinking. She should have thought of that. She'd seen rescue programs on TV about vehicles catching fire. She grabbed Ernie's good arm and wrapped it around her shoulder. Then she part slid, part walked him down the slope to the clearing. Her breath rasped like a dull saw in dry wood. She helped the old man sit down.

Ernie leaned against a deadfall elm stump and heaved a big sigh. " 'The best laid schemes of mice and men gang aft a-gley,' Robert Burns said. A heck of a start to a fishing trip, eh?"

"This is no time for poetry. I don't know what you had in mind, Ernie, but we're in deep trouble here." She clambered to the truck, rescued her sportsbag, and hauled it to the clearing. She took a big bandaid, peeled the papers off, and covered the cut on Ernie's head, dabbing at the blood on his shirt with a rag.

"Where's the field hospital, sergeant? Call the medics."

Jess plunked on the damp grass beside Ernie, took scissors and first aid supplies to her own injuries, biting her lip as she cut back the jeans from the sore knee where the blood-soaked fabric was sticking to her leg.

"Not very good at that, are you, princess?"

Jess winced and concentrated on finishing her work. She applied muscle ointment to her sore

70

calves. The stupid old man had nearly gotten them killed and here he was criticizing her. Finished with her first aid work, she turned to Ernie with her face in a deep scowl much like her mom's when Jess had been mouthy. The old man had dozed off. For crying out loud, Ernie had gone to sleep.

10. Keep the
Home Fires Burning

A police car was parked in front of the Mather house when Brian and his dad pulled into the driveway. Brian ran up the back steps and into the kitchen. Jess's mother was making coffee. Her usually smiling face was grim, her skin the colour of uncooked pastry.

"Any news?" he asked.

His dad came in behind him, strode over and took Naomi Baines in his arms. "We've come to help."

Jess's mother sobbed into Sonny Dille's wide shoulder. "Nobody knows where they've gone."

"I bet Ernie's gone fishing. Jess would try to stop him." Brian said. He could remember back a few years when Ernie and Jess and he had been a team. "Ernie was happiest fishing."

"I wish it was that simple, Brian." His dad

gave him one of his go-away-kid looks and led Naomi over to the kitchen table.

Naomi wiped the tears from her face with Sonny's large spotless handkerchief.

Ruth Mather, red in the face, her agitated voice louder than usual, was talking to two uniformed police officers in the living room. She was leafing through a photo album, trying to find a recent shot of Ernie. Brian thought of the one he had tucked in the corner of his dresser mirror, the one of the three of them holding their last catch of fish proudly, all of them wearing their Alberta Dairy Pool tractor hats, and he, Brian, with his on backwards, trying to look like a cool kid. Happy days. It had been taken two years ago, before Ernie was having real problems remembering everything, before Brian and Jess had stopped being friends. What had gone wrong?

Brian stood there in a kind of trance, watching and listening to all the grownups talking. Sonny comforting Naomi and talking about what to do, Ruth and the police discussing where Ernie might have gone, getting a description of the truck. The air around them hummed with panic. He had to move.

"I'm not leaving here until we know where they are for sure," Ruth said. "He might phone. If I don't answer the phone, he could panic." She started polishing the coffee table, straightening the magazines.

Brian padded quietly down the stairs to Ernie's

shop, wishing with all his heart that the old man was down there in the musty shop. That was where they'd hung out when he'd been a little kid and Ernie had watched him after school. Ernie had his tools mounted neatly on plywood. Brian's child-sized tools still hung on a smaller board beside Ernie's. They hung silent and dusty on their outlined and painted shapes, a red toolbox open on the scarred workbench in front. Brian's throat tightened in a knot of memory and worry. He fished through the toolbox and found the pliers that were missing from their spot on the plywood. He put them back with care. Like Ernie, Brian put everything in its place. Today everything in his life was out of place.

Brian turned his attention to the beaten-up green metal two-drawer filing cabinet. Ernie kept good records — warranties for appliances, plans for birdhouses, a doghouse, all the different projects the three of them had built together. There were maps of Alberta, Calgary, Edmonton, Red Deer. Ernie always said there was no excuse for getting lost if you had a map.

Brian yanked out the bottom drawer. He wondered whether Ernie had known before any of them that he had Alzheimer's Disease. The old man had made maps of everywhere they'd fished. There should be a folder of detailed directions with notes about best bait, best lures, and types of fish available at their favourite fishing spots. Brian flipped through the files — Addresses, Appliances, Archives, Birdhouses, Building ideas, Camping spots, Directions, Disease, Finances, Fishing spots.... He pulled that file out. It was half empty. All the detailed maps of fishing spots up north were missing, as was the plastic folder that held the fishing licence and guidelines for season and catch limits and release rules. The poles and tackle box were gone too from their normal spot leaning in the corner by the laundry tubs. His box of crayons and markers, the pile of drawing paper, the tub of Lego, sat on the shelf gathering dust. How long had it been since he'd come over to play?

Brian sat back on his heels. He could hear the grownups mumbling upstairs, and the thump, creak, thump of pacing feet. The fingers of his left hand felt for his marble bag, the ancient leather pouch with its seven coins. How he wished it were a magic "poke," only it wasn't gold he wanted to find, it was Ernie and Jess. What if they had an accident? What if they went off the road, or hit another car? He gulped.

He could have prevented it. If he hadn't been doing somersaults. If he hadn't been showing off, he would have spotted Jess. Stupid kid! If anything bad happened to them! He banged his fist on the filing cabinet, skinning his knuckles. Some cool kid. Some smart dude. Nobody's laughing now. But nobody.

Could Brian talk his dad into going to hunt for Jess and Ernie? He couldn't go alone. He couldn't stop his awfulizer head from going crazy, seeing all sorts of blood and bad things — smashed cars, drowning bodies, freezing limbs.

All of them making Ernie and Jess deader than the dead cat Midas. They needed rescuing, that was for sure. He shivered.

Curiosity moved his fingers to the file marked Directions and the one marked Disease. He glanced up the stairs to make sure he was alone. Maybe Ernie had moved some of the maps to Directions. He had to find out where the two of them had gone. Strange that Ruth hadn't sent the police down here already. She was usually so practical. He'd never seen her so flustered. Maybe she had an awfulizer head too. But then again, Jess and Ernie might be just at the giant mall and some security guard would spot them, or Jess would phone.

A pile of yellow lined foolscap pages with Ernie's neat small handwriting fell out. Brian glanced through the pages.

How to make coffee—fill pot with eight cups of water. Pour into machine. Put filter in plastic basket. Put four tablespoons of real coffee in filter. Turn on coffee maker. When finished coffee make sure machine is turned off. Light goes off when machine is turned off at little switch beside the dial on the left side.

There were directions for how to make tea, toast, fried eggs, and hot chocolate. Notes on one page were short and sharp.

Ruth is my wife. She likes sugar in her coffee but not in tea.

Shave every day.

The Anglican church is three blocks away.

(Keep map in jacket pocket.)

I go to a Seniors choir on Thursday afternoons at 1:30 pm. Ruth drives me.

(Don't ask about this too often. She gets mad.)

There are seven days in a week. Keep calendar with me.

Brian shoved the sheets of paper back into the folder. His stomach flip-flopped. As he pushed the folder back into the filing cabinet, the one marked Disease slipped off his knee and the contents spilled onto the floor. There were brochures and booklets and information sheets all about Alzheimer's Disease. An envelope with Ruth's name on it leaned against his blue-jeaned leg. He picked it up.

"To be opened in case of my incapacity or disappearance."

Brian flung it back into the folder along with all the material. He was about to close the cabinet when the phone rang. He automatically lifted the receiver.

"Is that you, Jess? Where are you?"

"Hi, I'm Mark Saunders, a reporter with the Landis Leader. I'm phoning for more information about Ernie Mather and the girl he has with him." The voice was young.

"Hello, Mather house. Brian Dille speaking."

A police officer upstairs interrupted. "Excuse me, unless you have information related to the disappearance of Ernie Mather, please get off the line."

"A truck driver going through Landis reported

seeing his camper on Main Street. He was hogging the road. So I thought his wife would like to know."

"Thanks very much. From now on please contact your local RCMP detachment. The family needs the line free." The police officer's voice was brusque and unfriendly. Brian felt sorry for the young reporter. The guy upstairs hung up.

Before Mark went off the line Brian blurted, "If my Dad and I come up there, would you help us find Ernie?"

"Who are you?"

"Ernie's an old friend of mine. He's got Alzheimer's and Jess is probably trying to keep him safe."

"Brian, are you down there?" His dad's voice echoed in the stairwell.

"See you, Mark." Brian hung up the phone. "I'm coming."

"What were you doing?" His father's black eyes peered into the gloomy basement. The hinged lamp attached to the workbench cast an eerie creamy light over Brian curled on the floor by the filing cabinet and the phone.

"Reading his files. Trying to figure out where Ernie and Jess have gone." He shook his head. "He's been having a hard time for a long time, Dad. He didn't let on. He acted like everything was all right. He even had directions written here for how to make coffee, and he used to cook up a storm." Brian blinked back tears. He didn't know how his dad felt about twelve-year-old boys crying. He didn't know how his dad felt about much of anything.

"Someone spotted the truck on Highway Two heading north. A driver with a cell phone called the RCMP to report, saying he thought the driver was drunk, he was driving so erratically. And they've been seen in Landis. I thought Ruth hid the keys." Brian's dad flipped on the overhead light. He was standing with his huge hands held out, pinkish palms forward, a look of questioning on his serious face.

"Some kid reporter phoned from Landis. The police told him to get off the line. I talked to him though."

"What did he say?"

"He didn't have time to say much. They're up there though."

"So, what are you saying?"

"I can't stay here. If I hadn't been such a goof...."

"It's not your fault, Brian."

"Couldn't we drive up and look for them? I know all our old hangouts. I don't want to stay here."

"You said that." His father was rubbing his chin thoughtfully. The two of them headed up the steps. "Not much hope of selling insurance policies on a long weekend...."

"And Mom's away."

"As usual." Brian's dad paused. "Naomi and Ruth are talking about going up with the police. Ruth is packing a few things. She doesn't want to leave until someone is here. A friend from the church is coming. Ernie or Jess might call or come back. One of Naomi's friends will take over at Jess's house."

"So can we go? Right now? You could give your cellular phone a real workout."

"True, but—"

"Can we go, Dad, can we?"

"I'm not much of a camper," Brian's dad chuckled. "I've become a real city boy."

"There's a cheap motel on the south side of town. We could stay there."

Dad was so funny. Didn't like the outdoors. Didn't want to dress casual. It was like he was allergic to the country. For a guy who was raised in Trinidad and cut sugar cane before he'd gone away to school, it was pretty weird. Well, Brian, boy, you'll have to watch your step. You need your dad along so you can make this trip. And it was imperative to make this trip.

He had to find Jess and Ernie — before it was too late.

11. In the Woods

Jess rummaged through the debris strewn around the camper. The sun on her head was hot, the breeze cool. It must be mid-afternoon and she was starved. Two pesky mosquitoes danced before her eyes. She rescued a jar of sugar and a pretty sunflower-painted can of tea bags from a patch of deep green moss where they had flown when the camper broke apart. Grandma Ruth's stretched woolly cardigan lay in a heap at the base of a rotting poplar. She found a jar of instant coffee, a blue enamel coffee pot, a tin of matches, two candles, and thank goodness — sleeping bags, camping pillows, and blankets in a big green duffel bag that had rolled under a dogwood bush. Everything was scattered like toys in an abandoned nursery.

A woodpecker hammered on the crumpled

roof, making a tinny racket. Stupid bird. Jess laughed in spite of herself. He wouldn't get any treats out of the ruined camper. Maybe he was showing off or proclaiming his territory to neighbouring rivals. Look what I've got, guys.

The smell of damp earth churned by the crashing camper, plus an overpowering odour of crushed leaves, roots, and grasses, filled Jess's nose. She coughed. Her shoulders and neck hurt — and her knees. Her right knee had jammed under the dashboard as the truck careened down the hill. She shivered, wrapped Grandma Ruth's sweater around her. It smelled faintly of Ruth's cologne, and Jess was stabbed with loneliness sharper than any of her aches and pains. She longed for safety and for her mom and Ruth. She shook herself and plunked down on a hummock of wild grass and strawberry blossoms, still clutching the jar of sugar and the fancy tin of tea.

Ernie was curled like a baby under the bright green sleeping bag she had pulled out of the wreck and wrapped around him. His left hand hung limp on the cover, a bluebottle fly walking sedately on its pale freckled surface. The bump on his head had turned blue, but it wasn't as bad as Jess had first thought. His breathing rasped louder than the woodpecker's beak on dead aspen.

There was definitely something the matter with Ernie. He was having a really hard time moving. His joints must be stiff and painful. An old man like him could break bones easily. He'd started coughing and wheezing, and Jess was afraid he was catching a cold. His voice when he had cried out to her had sounded croaky, like his throat had a permanent frog in it. This was no place for Ernie.

"Don't leave me here alone. Please!" he had said over and over again as she had struggled up the slope and down, rescuing things from the truck cab and the destroyed camper.

She had her survival kit by her side and a plastic bag with fruit strip and granola bar wrappers, two empty juice boxes, and other little bits of garbage from their little lunches so far.

Suddenly, as suddenly as the accident itself, Jess felt cold, colder than an ice cube, colder than standing inside the walk-in refrigerator in the school cafeteria. She wanted to cry, but she had forgotten how to. Her eyes were scratchy, her skin clammy, her throat tight. She was having trouble thinking, shaking so hard she had to clutch her knees. Huddled there on the hummock of grass, Jess rocked back and forth, back and forth. A few tears escaped, rolled down her cheeks and dried in the breeze from the river. Her head hurt. Ernie moaned in his sleep.

"I have to get organized." Jess was not alone. She was responsible for Ernie. She had to keep Ernie safe. "But you've gotten us into a terrible spot, you stupid old man." The sound of her own voice in the noisy woods eased the loneliness.

The eastern bank of the Athabasca River

above Landis was very high and steep, steeper than some places on the North Saskatchewan in the city. In some places it was as steep as a staircase and in other places it sloped like a wheelchair ramp. Here on this particular stretch of the bank, it seemed to have three ridges, like three landings on the stairs of a very tall house. The truck had stopped at the edge of the first ridge. Jess planned to set up camp on the second ridge, away from the camper debris, where there was a fairly flat plain about the size of a ball diamond. The flat area was filled with saskatoon bushes, dogwood brush, and old beaten-down grass. Then the bank dropped away again and sloped to the last abrupt ridge above the river.

She picked her way down a deer path towards the river below, glancing up and down the shore warily, watching for animals. The wide cold brownish river hurried past, rolling over round rocks coated with slime and weeds. Whitecaps rippled around a massive boulder halfway out to a heavily wooded island. The river hummed an unfamiliar tune. Waves splashing against driftwood. No people. No animals. Nothing but a wet and squishy clay beach with bleached rocks and tree trunks, and large paw prints going away from her into the rushing current. Some creature had been here and left. Bear?

She stared into the river, saw rocks and boulders coated with moss and silt on the bottom, a school of minnows. Her head felt dizzy. It was like the river in her nightmare. It looked dangerous, and yet it beckoned her. Just fall in, float away. I'll carry you back to civilization. Sure, or drown me, thought Jess.

The sun slid towards the western horizon. She and Ernie were stranded on the mighty Athabasca River, one of Canada's longest and most historic waterways. Funny she should think of that; she'd heard a Canadian geographer talk about "When Our Rivers Were Our Roads," and it had stuck in her mind. He'd visited their class because he and Mrs. Slater were old school friends. Too bad the river wasn't a road any more. Every year people drowned in rivers in Alberta. It didn't matter that they were closer to Landis by water than by road. There was no way she was going into that river. No way. She was no voyageur, no early explorer. She didn't want her nightmare coming true.

Besides, she still had Shank's Mare, which was Ernie's name for feet. Good old Ernie. They'd had so many good times together. She was really mad at this disease for taking him away in bits and pieces. Maybe it was better to go like Midas and never know what hit you. She sighed and stared around her, trying to get her bearings, trying to stop the sadness inside about her dead cat. Part of her heart felt like she would never be happy again.

Across the river, meadows ran right down to the shore. The clay banks were lower. A flock of Canada Geese honked from the driftwood-covered tip of the island. Jess could see no power lines, phone lines, or smoke from chimneys. When she strained her ears she could hear the sound of traffic. Surely there was a road on the other side of the river, behind the rolling fields and poplar windbreak. She had seen farms with No Trespassing, No Hunting, and Rural Crime Watch signs posted on trees and fenceposts — but that had been many miles back. She'd seen skinny rutted gas well roads, but no trucks. They were in a wilderness area, probably Crown land belonging to the government. No one came here for anything — except maybe guys on all-terrain vehicles out for a wild roar in the woods, and she didn't want to meet anyone like that. She'd gotten scared once when the three of them had gone camping at Lawrence Lake. Two guys had circled their campsite, screaming and throwing beer bottles, until Ernie had told them he'd report them. That was back when Ernie could still sound like a school principal, an Army lieutenant. She and Brian had been glad they'd had him as their champion. Now each of them was alone. So very much alone.

She made her way back up from the beach to the edge of the lowest ridge. A red slash on a dead black poplar marked this excuse for a beach. Someone must come here to fish. There were charred logs, rusted tin cans, and a few scorched rocks in a ring. How she wished they'd choose today to come. But it wasn't likely. May was early to be out camping.

Jess followed the deer path up and over the

second ridge to the grassy hummock close to Ernie, catching her breath. Her knee hurt. The backs of her legs throbbed. Climbing ladders would be easier. Her ears had picked up more sounds as she came away from the river. Trucks on that so-distant road, gearing down for a hill. Sound carried a long way when you were in a river valley like this. Too bad she wasn't Tarzan or Jane, she could swing across and get them rescued. But the river was far too wide for that. What a dreamer!

"Hello! Is there anyone there?" Jess shouted. "Help! We need help!" No sounds came back. Jess felt more alone than a polar bear on an ice floe.

Sitting on the wet ground with the sea of green plants surrounding her, the melodies of invisible songbirds above, the creaking of dead branches and strange muffled sounds of unrecognizable things across the river, made Jess shiver. She was dizzy, light-headed, like when you wake from a dream and get up too quickly. Only this was no dream. She didn't know what frightened her most — being lost, being alone, being afraid of what she couldn't see, or being stupid and scaring her mom. A flood of bad thoughts tumbled in her head like the muddy Athabasca racing over rocks in the river.

"Okay, sergeant, it's up to you to get us out of this fix." Jess heard Ernie's voice in her mind as if he was right beside her giving her instructions in one of their games, not lying there in his sleeping bag snoring. "Keep a cool head in an emergency. Follow the rules and keep busy, so you don't have time to stew and panic. Fear is a killer. Panic is fear's brother."

Jess stood up, placing the precious supply of tea and sugar on a wide flat rock beside her survival kit, threw her shoulders back and struggled up the hill towards the camper. First she had to set up camp, make sure they had shelter, food, and water. She had work to do.

12. Ernie Forgets

"Help! Help me, someone," Ernie called. He pulled himself up to a sitting position and stared wildly about, his right hand reaching out, the knobby knuckles of his fingers shaking. "Please don't leave me."

A young woman came clattering and banging her way into the clearing where he sat. "Did everyone get out alive? Were there any casualties?" He tugged at the sweater as the girl leaned down and tried to tuck him into his sleeping bag.

"That's Ruth's sweater. It's pure wool. Where's Ruth? What have you done with Ruth?" he cried. "I don't know where I am."

Ernie watched the girl work. She cleared a patch of earth, brought rocks to ring a firepit, broke fallen branches, made a teepee of twigs and birch bark. Whoever had taught her how to build a fire had done a good job.

"I'm glad you know bush craft, princess." He tilted his head slightly. "Do I know you? Are we all right?" His voice grated. His throat hurt. His whole body ached.

"I'm Jess, your next-door neighbour. We're fine, Ernie. We had fruit strips and juice for a snack earlier. It's like a picnic. You and I have gone on lots of picnics. We used to fish together when I was young. Brian Dille came with us. You remember him, don't you? You remember me. So we'll just pretend this is a camping trip. We'll have to wait for someone to find us, that's all. Don't worry."

"Are you a nurse?"

"I'm Jess. I live next door."

"Of course, you told me that."

She bent to tie up her sneaker.

"You're awfully young to be a nurse." Ernie tried to speak clearly in spite of his sore throat. "I don't like hospitals. I don't want to go to hospital."

"I know."

Ernie raised his eyes. His vision was cloudy and he shivered with cold. The dampness seeped through his clothes, even through the sleeping bag he'd bought at Camper's Village.

He could feel tears gathering again. He'd had an accident with the truck. He knew that much. It was embarrassing having this young woman looking after him. He should be looking after her. Chivalry was dead, with the last of the

Knights of the Round Table. He sighed, wiped his eyes with his left arm, wiped the tears away. Why wouldn't his body cooperate?

"You won't leave me here alone, will you?"

"I have to find more wood, Ernie. I'll be back before the kettle boils." She balanced the blue enamel camp kettle on a rock beside the hottest part of the fire. The lid rattled and flames scorched the side black. A giant raven cawed loudly overhead, scolding them for intruding. An echo came from across the river.

Ernie stared up into the treetops. " 'Consider the birds of the air, they toil not neither do they spin, but God takes care of them.' That's in the gospel of Luke, you know." So many people don't know the Bible these days, Ernie thought. Where did they get their comfort?

Ernie loved the aspen woods. He felt like he was in church. The trees were a cathedral, tall and stately, clinging to the hillside, shading the bushes, the flowering saskatoons, the wild roses, gooseberries, raspberries, the young willow. If it weren't for the troubles he was having with his body, with his brain, he'd feel at home.

"God will take care of us too." Ernie's voice filled with confidence. He began reciting comforting phrases. " 'The Lord is my shepherd, I'll not want.' " He leaned against the tree, staring at the girl. Suddenly he knew who she was. He remembered a game they played together. "Bert, is that you?"

Jess dropped the wood she had been

collecting, raced over and gave Ernie a hug. Elm seeds cascaded from his white hair. The woods were alive with spring growth. A brilliant yellow marsh buttercup gleamed in a patch of sunlight, brighter by far than the flames from their small fire. "It's so good to have you with me."

"How did we get here?"

"You were going fishing, Ernie. You drove off the road."

"Ruth will come. Ruth will come for us." He tried to raise his arms, but they ached so much he gave up. His left arm didn't work at all. That frightened him. His eyes on Jess's clouded with tears. "It's my fault, isn't it?"

He watched her through a veil of tears. She was working around the fire. She wrapped the long sleeve of the sweater around her hand and plucked the bubbling kettle from the edge of the firepit. She struggled with the lid. It was very hot. Ernie's hand stung in sympathy. She dumped in two tea bags and stirred the pot with a twig. She pulled a package of cookies out of her sportsbag, ripped the cellophane wrapper off with her teeth, and handed him three chocolate sandwiches and a plastic mug of tea with sugar stirred into it.

"Thank you very much. I like milk in my tea, don't I?"

"The milk carton burst when the camper smashed. The jam bottle broke on a rock. We've got buns and fish bait. I can't find the margarine or the honey."

" 'Behold, I will deliver to you a land of milk and honey.' " Ernie used his Scripture-quoting voice. Jess shook her head.

"I don't think this is what God had in mind, Ernie." The girl laughed and blew on her tea, dunked her cookie in the hot liquid. It reminded Ernie of his brother Pete. Pete dunked his cookies, his doughnuts, even his bread crusts. Was he dead?

He wished he had his files. He had written things in there to remember. But now he couldn't find the drawer. He wouldn't be able to read with his eyes so foggy. Besides he had come out here to do something about this sickness. What was it he meant to do?

13. The Hunt Begins

Brian and his dad pulled into Landis about three o'clock Friday afternoon. They parked on the main street beside the bank. Brian turned off the Beatles tape he and his dad had been listening to.

"Place seems awfully quiet," Brian's dad said.

The cellular phone rang. Brian jumped, surprised at hearing the low hum. His dad picked up the receiver.

"Sonny Dille here." He drummed his fingers on the dashboard as he listened to whoever was calling. Brian fished through the glove compartment for some change to buy a soft drink.

"I'm afraid not, Charlie. I'm out in the bush with my kid. The neighbour has gone and got lost. Taken the kid next door. So we're out here in the middle of nowhere...."

The voice on the other end interrupted the flow of words.

"No, it wasn't anything like that. The poor guy's losing it, you know. He doesn't even recognize his wife some days. The office was slow today, you know, holiday weekend and all. I came because Brian wanted to help. We all used to be friends. The girl's father did a bunk. Turned out he was a loser, drank like a fish. Somehow Marie and I never kept up with Naomi and Jess. Now the kid is out here somewhere with the old guy."

More talk. Brian's dad listened and polished the dashboard of his late model black four-by-four with his white handkerchief.

"Look, if the situation gets ugly here, I'll come back fast, believe me. Give Art my apologies, okay?" He hung up.

"I forgot, it's Art's stag tonight. He's getting remarried on Monday."

Brian sighed, bent and did up his shoe laces.

His dad shook his head and toured the streets of Landis looking for the newspaper office. "Pretty dinky town. It makes me nervous, being out here. I think it's a good thing to do, Brian, but I don't know enough about the bush. This isn't my country."

"It's mine though. It's just farms and lakes and the big river, Dad."

"Villages in Trinidad are different. I didn't bring the right clothes."

Brian studied his dad's face. "I've been out here plenty — with Ernie and Jess. I feel really safe out here. I don't get it."

His dad was clutching the wheel with both hands, driving slowly down the second side street. Two guys in pickups passed. They stared at the four-by-four and at Brian and his dad.

"Look, there's the newspaper office. They'll know where searchers are supposed to go." Brian pointed down the road to a dingy storefront office with a blue-and-white sign, "The Landis Leader — First with the news in the county."

When they walked in, a young guy that Brian figured was Mark Saunders was talking on the phone. His wide reddish face shone in the fluorescent light, glistening with sweat. Dark wavy hair hung nearly to his shoulders. He motioned to two chairs facing a cluttered table at the end of the room.

A slim teenaged girl with long black hair, dark eyes, and a smooth make-up-free face approached them. "Hi, I'm Holly. Mark has been expecting you. I'm working on this story with him. Coffee?"

After introductions, Brian and his dad sat down at the table covered with topographical maps. Holly brought a mug of coffee for Brian's dad and a carton of apple juice for Brian. A flip chart on an easel stood at the end of the table with a list of possible actions. Brian gulped the juice.

"This must be the most excitement the Landis Leader has had in years," Holly said. "Mark and I want to get the youth angle on this story. You know Jess well, Brian. Why do you think she went with Ernie? He wasn't a relative. I don't think most kids would do what she's doing. What's the story?"

Brian described how responsible Jess was, how lately she'd been really worried about Ernie. He even told her how he and Jess had been at odds, how he thought she should let Ernie go, how she had seemed extra mad at him at school lately and he didn't know why. Holly took notes on a clipboard with a pad of lined yellow paper. Her hair danced as she listened and wrote. Mark sipped a can of root beer.

Brian stopped talking suddenly, chewing his bottom lip, his hands shuffling papers on the table in front of him. He had probably said too much. He didn't want to look dumb. He was torn between saying more — trying to explain things — and being cool. He blinked.

"None of that personal stuff is for publication, Brian, don't worry," Mark said. "It's really helpful for us to fill in the background though."

Brian looked from Mark to Holly and down at the papers stacked in front of him. He put a paper clip on the corner to hold them together. "If I hadn't been being such an idiot, rolling on the lawn, I would have seen them. If Jess had been able to talk to me, she wouldn't have gone and done something so stupid and scary."

Holly put her clipboard down suddenly, reached out a hand and patted Brian's shoulder. "Losing touch with your friends is real hard, isn't it?"

A lump in Brian's throat threatened to burst. He stood quickly, nearly knocking over the chair, grabbed a doughnut and shoved it in his mouth, walked over to the window and stared briefly at the busy, unconscious, life-is-normal street. Then he turned to face the office.

"I should have stopped them."

"I told Brian it wasn't his fault," Sonny Dille said. "He's some upset, man."

The phone rang. Holly answered it, cradling the receiver between her ear and her shoulder while she took notes.

"Ernie's wife Ruth and Naomi, Jess's mother, are on their way up here with a police escort. Ruth wouldn't leave until someone arrived to 'keep the home fires burning,' whatever that means," Holly said. "Ruth is an Olnichuk. My parents know them. Dad went to school with her brother. He has the family farm out the Landis Trail road."

"That sounds like Ruth. She'd be convinced that Ernie would come home. At least up here she'll have her brother's family to keep her company. What about Naomi, though? How must she feel? Jess has been missing for most of the day." Brian studied his dad's face. His father was going through something here, but he couldn't figure out what. Maybe his dad was an awfulizer too. Sonny Dille poured himself another cup of coffee from the pot in the corner. Stacks of last week's newspaper leaned precariously by the door. Stale odours of cigarettes, newsprint, and ink permeated the room.

Holly fastened four detailed maps together on the wall behind the table.

She put red tacks on the places where Ernie and Jess had been spotted.

"Several drivers phoned to complain about an old guy driving erratically. He preferred the middle of the road. We haven't heard anything more since noon." The small flags were dotted along Highway Two all the way to Landis. There were none after.

"Where have they gone?" Mark asked. He was working at one of the word processors.

"Probably to one of our fishing spots," Brian said. "You better mark Calling Lake, Island Lake, Baptiste, and Lawrence. We fished off the bridge up by Smith on the Athabasca once because Ernie heard there were giant pickerel lurking there. But Jess didn't like that. She's afraid of rivers."

"I thought there was no public access to Island Lake. More's the pity." Holly shook her head. "Can you own a lake?"

Brian looked at the teenager. "Ernie knew a bush pilot with a cottage. He let us park in his lane. We launched from his dock."

"Don't mind Holly, she's going through a cynical phase." Mark moved to the flip chart, turned to a fresh sheet and wrote down the names of the lakes. "Okay, we know the who, the why, the how, and the when, we just have to narrow down the where. Say a little more about those lakes, Brian."

"The fishing is really good at Baptiste by the Narrows." Brian walked over and pointed to the skinny part of Baptiste Lake. "That's where I caught my first pickerel." Watching Holly and Mark work at getting the story fascinated him. All the stuff the Language Arts teacher had said about good investigative reporting was true. He just hoped they wouldn't find a tragedy at the end of the search.

"There's an all-points bulletin out. There's search parties from the Forest Service, the Scouts and Venturers, and the RCMP." Holly chomped a sugar-coated doughnut. Sprinkles of white cascaded down her black T-shirt. "Hopefully we'll hear something before sunset. We've got a very unsettled weather situation this weekend. Possible thunderstorms with hail. Frost warnings for low-lying areas."

"I want to try Baptiste," Brian bounced up and down on his runners. "It's got good access. Dad and I could start there."

"I don't know about this, son," Brian's dad said. "These people seem to have things in hand. They're used to this wilderness stuff. Bugs, bears, the whole bit. You've helped already, giving them the locations. Maybe we should call it a day, head back to the city."

"Oh, Dad, give me a break!' Brian shouted. "We just got here. We haven't done anything yet. I'm staying until I find them."

"Hold it right there, kid." Sonny sprang to his feet and grabbed Brian by the arm. "Boys don't talk like that to their fathers. You've developed a big mouth, boy. That's probably why Jess is having such a struggle with you. Who do you think you are, anyway?"

Man and boy stood toe to toe, the man towering over the boy, his hand clamped on Brian's wrist, both frozen in the unfamiliar violent stance. Brian's mind was whirring like a video game at high speed. He pulled his hand away.

"We're all pretty nervous and scared here," said Mark quietly. "Why don't you take some deep breaths and talk this through?"

Brian gulped. "It's just that no one else knows Ernie and Jess like I do, Dad. He and Jess and I had some great times together. I owe him for that. I owe him for lots of things. He's been a real buddy, taught me all about living in the bush. I kind of forgot that for awhile after he got sick. I'm scared. He could be hurt or worse." Brian could feel the awfulizer in him going berserk. They could be dead, it said. "He's been closer to me than anyone."

His father pulled himself up to his full six feet, his broad shoulders back, his eyes dark and hidden. Something in his face looked sad, sadder than Jess at Midas's funeral.

Looking at his dad's face, Brian realized how that last remark must have sounded. But it had been true. Ernie had been closer to him than anyone, including his father. He gulped and said, "I need you to help, you've got the great wheels

101

and that new cellular phone. You could keep in touch with the office and the RCMP by phone."

Brian's dad turned and stared at him. Brian kept pushing. "We could check into the motel, buy some bug dope, maybe even buy you some serious camping clothes, and head out to the highway right away."

"It could get nasty, Brian. After typhoons and storms, I had to help clean up the beaches in Trinidad. I saw some pretty gruesome sights. I can't understand you young kids, wanting to watch horror on television, read horror stories in books. When you've seen death and tragedy up close, that stuff pales. It hurts you to see real death, confront real pain. I don't want anything bad to happen to you. I don't want you getting hurt...."

"Brian's a big boy, now, Mr. Dille, maybe he needs to see for himself. You can't protect him forever," Holly interrupted. "He needs to be doing this. He's the one with inside knowledge. Nobody else has the slightest idea where they are."

Mr. Dille scratched his chin thoughtfully. He shook himself like a dog shedding water.

"This kid, man. This kid of mine. He's driven, you know what I mean? Stubborn as a mule, like my granpappy. I vowed I'd never go back-country again in my lifetime. Now, here I go." He shook his head, tossed his hands in the air. "Following my son."

"Way to go, Mr. Dille," said Mark.

It was the longest speech Brian had ever

heard his dad give. He didn't say anything. He just went over and stood close beside him, close enough to smell his expensive cologne. The storm between them had passed. His dad's arm went round Brian's shoulder, and Brian felt the warmth. With his dad's help, he could do anything. He felt the resolve to find Jess and Ernie strengthen. There was hope.

Holly phoned the RCMP and discovered that no one had heard or seen anything more. There was a gathering of all the volunteer searchers in the parking lot of the Safeway store at five p.m. Brian's dad phoned and registered at the Riverview motel. Then the four of them went to the meeting.

"All these people. Who would have thought?" Holly sounded surprised. Brian was pleased to see the crowds.

14. Setting Up Camp

Jess had found matches in a tin under the cushion, so she'd been able to light the fire. She'd made tea, nearly burning her hand on the old kettle, and added branches to the flames. Ernie had wakened and they'd had a little visit. She hadn't found the hatchet or the bow saw yet, so she kept piling small stuff on the fire. Maybe she should forage further and find a dry stump. She had to think about shelter for the night. The cab of the truck was on such a slant it would not be comfortable. The camper was destroyed. She rose to hunt for more wood, stretch her legs, and study the situation.

In some ways she envied Ernie sitting there praying. She had gone with him to the cathedral some times. It was peaceful, comforting, seemed to help keep life in perspective. Ernie called it keeping in touch with God. Her mom didn't go to church. Naomi Baines worked so hard with people all the time that she liked to take Sundays to have a quiet time, sleep in, maybe go on a picnic, for a ride in the country, or out to brunch with Jess.

Unless someone found them soon, Jess wouldn't be going anywhere with anyone. So much for their long weekend together in Banff, up in the mountains hiking.

A picture of her mother and Grandma Ruth flashed into her head. They were pacing the floor in the Mather kitchen, a police officer talking on the phone. Anxious looks, tears, wringing hands. Jess felt sorry for them, for what she was afraid was going on at home, but she couldn't let herself think about them, she had to think about herself and Ernie. She found two fallen birches and hauled them to the fire. She broke them up by stomping on them with her good leg. Pieces of wood flew everywhere. It took so long to do everything. Her knee hurt all the time. Sweat poured down her face, mosquitoes hovered. One bit her temple. She swatted it so hard her head hurt. She fished out the bug ointment, put some on, put a band-aid on a scratch on her hand. Boy, was she glad she had a survival kit in her sportsbag. Maybe now she could make her mom understand.

What about wild animals? What about bad weather? What if Ernie got worse or wandered away? What about her mother and Grandma

Ruth hunting for them?

Did everyone have a head that stewed about how other people were feeling, and who was to blame and how could you help, and how could you keep from worrying so much? Sometimes she couldn't sleep for worrying about people — like Ernie — and when things got really bad at school she'd remember that her dad had left. Maybe that was her fault too. She chewed her lip. Too bad she couldn't put a sportsbag in her head to store everything in compartments. Life would be easier.

If she had a sportsbag in her head she could learn to meditate, maybe cook or garden to work things through. Only ten minutes allowed for worrying about Ernie, or ten minutes about wanting her work neat no matter what.

Ernie prayed, her mother practiced yoga, and Grandma Ruth said her meditation came with a trowel attached. She worked in her garden and knitted giant sweaters for everyone. Brian used to draw or make things in Ernie's shop. His parents always seemed to be out with friends.

Jess brought over two blankets she had rescued from the camper and a ball of rope. She strung a piece of rope between the tree Ernie was leaning on and a skinny birch. With her Swiss Army knife she cut lengths of rope and tied the corners of the blanket to four trees. The rope between Ernie's tree and the birch acted as a roof peak. Jess attached the other blanket behind this makeshift tent as a shelter. She had discovered some thin plastic rolled in the smashed cupboard and attached it to the blankets with clothespins to keep out rain and wind.

Ernie watched from his tree, his eyes large, round, a frown creasing his forehead. He was reciting beautiful words in a clear whisper. " 'Sing a new song, make a joyful noise all the earth. Let the seas roar. Let the floods clap their hands: let the hills be joyful together.' "

Jess sighed. Those words must be from the Bible. They were comforting, but still she worried.

Jess ran to the edge of the little clearing, stared down through the trees to the silt-filled current. It was a cold, forbidding, ancient river. It frightened her. Yet she felt pulled towards it as if it held secrets she wanted to know. A pair of hawks circled and swooped, disappeared behind dark pines on the far side of the rushing current.

"That river was the highway to the north in the old days, you know. Pioneers and coureurs de bois used it to travel up and down." Ernie said.

Jess nodded her head—she'd heard this before, from Ernie and from the geographer who had come to her class.

"The landing by the town is where people loaded their goods to go to Fort Edmonton. There's an old trail runs all the way to St. Albert. It's empty now. The river is deserted most of the time too. We travel on highways, fly in planes. The mighty Athabasca carries sludge from pulp mills, dead trees, runoff from fertilized fields, and the occasional fishing boat or canoeist. The fish have too much mercury, so we can't eat them."

"A couple wouldn't hurt us, would they?" Jess had rescued the fishing poles and frozen bait. "Can you walk?"

Ernie pulled himself up by gripping the tree with his right hand and kneeling on his right leg. Jess wrapped his left arm around her shoulder and the two of them manoeuvered their way down the path to the small beach. Behind the old tree with the red paint mark on it, close to the rock-strewn shore, they spotted two old folding summer chairs with sagging yellow webbing.

"Someone must use this place. You can watch for them, Ernie — while you fish." Jess helped Ernie to sit in the lawn chair. Its legs were weak, but Ernie wasn't a heavy man. She handed him his fishing pole, put a minnow on his hook, and tossed it in the river. She made sure his sore left hand was resting on the chair arm and his right was free to hold the fishing rod. When she was a little girl, just after her father had left home, she and Ernie and Brian had gone fishing at Half Moon Lake, before the green algae had gotten too bad. Ernie had baited the hook, taught her how to hold the rod, schooled both kids on sitting still in the boat. Now she was helping Ernie.

"This is Crown land, you know. All the rivers in Alberta have public land along the shorelines so the wildlife have access to water and food. That's why I love this province. That's why I love Canada."

"Yes, Ernie, I know." She was glad he was making sense. When he didn't, it made her tight in the stomach and dry in the mouth. "I do too."

Now Jess could finish setting up camp. It must be past supper time. From the vantage of the beach, she studied the opposite shoreline. She could hear the water rushing over rocks. In some ways the river was company itself, flowing, chattering, hurrying along, busy like another person. Was a person ever really alone by a river? As long as you didn't have to travel on it or swim in it.

Ernie slumped over his fishing rod, dozing. His tractor cap was pulled down, shading his face. The sky had darkened. A stray bee buzzed by his right hand, but not in a stinging mood. Jess sprayed his hat and his hands with bug dope. Then she dug into her "survival kit" and brought out another snack. She opened a strip of fruit and chewed as she climbed up to the campsite.

The fire was dying. She'd have to find more wood. She went back down to the beach and hauled up three fairly hefty pieces of driftwood, threw two on the fire, and laid one close by for later. All this travelling up and down to the river was wearing her out. She wished they'd landed on a piece of prairie instead of this steep river bank.

Jess toured the wreck of the camper, the smashed truck, and the trampled bushes again in a desperate search for more foodstuffs and camping equipment. She found two skinny mattresses beside a giant fallen pine tree. A tin of corned beef and a jar of coffee creamer leaned against a poplar stump. She put them with the rest of the food. What she wouldn't give for the hatchet or the bow saw. She'd watched Ernie saw up thin birch fast. Birch made a good fire, but breaking it over her knee had made her left knee hurt as much as her right, the one she'd caught under the dash. It might get very cold tonight. There might be bears or coyotes out there, and a good fire would keep them away.

Should she go back to the road and try to find help? How far was it to the nearest farm? If only she'd paid more attention as they bumped and joggled along that dirt track. Should she make a big fire to attract attention? But fire could get out of control so easily. Then finally there was the river. If the inflatable boat was in the wreckage, she could take them out that way. She shivered, remembering the rushing river of her dream and the mighty Athabasca swirling below.

Bang! Crash! Noises in the woods to the south. Jess's heart thundered in her chest. The birds stopped singing. No breeze stirred the leaves, no twig snapped. She peered around the corner of an old black poplar with fungi shaped like saucers attached every few feet up its near side. She could see nothing but the startling green of new growth. She blinked and strained her eyes. Nothing moved.

I am not alone. I share these woods with others. Was that an elk, a moose, or a bear? She gulped. A deer wouldn't make that much racket. Elk or moose she could get out of the road of, but bears might be a different matter. Suddenly, memories of bad movies on late night TV with nasty men in dark woods flooded into her mind. She shook her head in an effort to send them away. She hugged the tree, felt the bark bite into her palm. A slight breeze rustled the leaves.

Don't be a silly goose, she told herself. This is northern Alberta. Nobody's going to hurt you. Whatever was out there had gone away or lain down to sleep. Get on with setting up camp.

Inside the makeshift tent, she rolled out the camper mattresses and the sleeping bags and plumped up the expandable pillows. It looked quite cosy. Just to be safe, she put rain gear and boots from the broken clothes cupboard into the shelter as well.

Jess took one last look around the crash site. That's when she spotted the yellow vinyl inflatable boat partially hidden under a crumpled piece of white aluminum camper siding. She hauled it out into the open and stared at it, waves of nausea rising in her throat. She hoped she wouldn't have to use the boat. It wasn't designed for rivers, was it? Just quiet fishing lakes.

Jess had a quick memory of herself and Brian and Ernie scrunched in that boat three years ago. That floppy boat had barely held the three of them then, and it was hard to paddle. She chucked it at the base of the marked tree along with its two plastic paddles and the foot pump.

Ernie was singing hymns.

Jess whistled under her breath as she pumped air into the boat. The sun sank below the orange and lilac sky behind the western hills. The northern sky looked dark and stormy. She helped Ernie up the bank to the campsite. The ravens scolded her continually and the hawks circled overhead, one bold sparrow chasing the giant hawk's tail.

She was afraid that no trace of the truck camper's route to the river would show unless someone looked very closely and spotted a tire skid, a bent birch, or a broken saskatoon, its blossoms crushed. Besides, she had heard no cars, only noises from heavy trucks across the impossibly wide river. The current was too fast for a boat to cross. The old Ernie would have known how fast the river was flowing.

She and Ernie camped above the Athabasca might be the only people in the world. If anyone was hunting for them, they were doing it quietly or the hunt was focused in a different direction. Probably they were dragging the lakes. On TV, they always dragged lakes for missing persons. But this wasn't TV or a book, it was real life.

15. Brian, the Hunter

"What possessed Jess?" Sonny Dille asked as he and Brian drove up the highway and turned into the park at Baptiste Lake after the five o'clock meeting in the parking lot. It was still light, thanks to being up north.

Then he answered the question for himself. "In all ways but one Jess is a normal kid. Most kids are pretty self-centred, but Jess has an overwhelming desire to help others. I think she grew up too fast after her dad did a bunk, I mean, since her father left. He had problems. You were too young to notice, Brian. It made Jess a worrier. She tries to read people's minds and figure out when they need something. She'd go with Ernie to protect him, to keep him company."

Brian nodded and gazed out the window. "We parked in that spot often." He swiveled his head to keep the boat launch in view.

113

The car pulled onto the beach, close to the shore. Two guys were cleaning fish. The waves lapped on the beach. A blue heron flew off, its long legs dangling like chopsticks.

"I wish it was Jess and Ernie there instead of a pair of fishermen," Sonny said. He sat behind the wheel of his jeep, stroking his chin.

Brian stared at the two men with tackle boxes open beside them on the picnic table. He hopped out and went over, asked them if they had seen Jess and Ernie, or the old camper. They shook their heads in unison.

"Kids who have an alcoholic parent grow up too fast," Sonny sighed. "They keep trying to fix things. Make things nice. I know what that's like."

Brian scratched his head. His dad seemed to be taking a journey all of his own. "You've never drunk a lot, Dad."

Brian couldn't remember ever being out with his dad for this length of time on his own. Each member of his family went their own way. His mom with her friends. His dad with his buddies. And Brian — since Ernie and Jess — who did he spend time with, talk to? The guys were all right to play with, but they didn't talk. Not like Ernie had. He missed Ernie.

He looked at his dad's big clean hands resting on the steering wheel. It was strange. His dad had immigrated to Canada from Trinidad to go to university. He had met and married Brian's mom. He'd never been back to Trinidad, wouldn't talk much about it. Didn't talk much about anything.

"Don't you get homesick for Trinidad?"

"Homesick?"

"I was thinking that Ernie was homesick for the old days, back when he was okay."

"You're a funny kid, Brian."

"Sometimes. The kids laugh at my jokes."

"No, I mean funny-strange."

"So, do you...get homesick? I want to go to Trinidad some day. When we did our family tree in grade four, I got really curious." Then Brian stopped talking. He remembered that his dad didn't talk about Trinidad much and had told him to forget it.

Sonny sighed. "I ran away...not like Ernie. I knew what I was doing. I wanted to get out, go somewhere else, become a different kind of person. I chose Canada. Going back would be hard. But I'd like to see my mom. She won't travel on airplanes. All these years I've tried to keep my past separate from my life now, my new family, city, job, and friends. Now, out here scouring the countryside for Jess and Ernie, I'm getting homesick for Trinidad."

"Let's walk, Dad. We can watch for signs of the camper, signs of them fishing." Brian opened the car door. "Maybe when everyone is safe we could go to Trinidad? But first we've got to find the runaways."

"Isn't this private property? Won't people ask questions? And my shoes aren't built for this."

"Dad, please?"

"When I was a kid growing up in Trinidad, we

had a little farm. I took care of the pig. I hated that pig. I hated the muck and mud in the yard. It stank. I swore I'd never be a farmer. I'd never cut sugar cane." Brian's father sprayed himself up and down with bug spray before they set out.

They hunted for signs of Ernie or Jess until the light started to fade in the sky. Brian's dad walked as if he was trying to keep the dirt off his shoes. Both of them were weary and discouraged as they drove back into Landis.

Thunder crashed. Lightning flashed across the sky to the south. Sonny rolled up the windows of the jeep. Rain spattered the windshield.

"This landscape is so different than Trinidad. It makes my head hurt. When I first got to Canada I thought I would freeze to death, and the prairies were so dry. A big change for a poor boy from the Caribbean. I washed the soil off my skin. I washed the grime from under my nails. I washed the smell of poverty away. I do not want to get to know this country too well. It makes me feel vulnerable. Like Jess and Ernie."

Brian gazed at his dad. His father concentrated on the road, but Brian figured his father wasn't seeing much of Alberta's northern roads. He was thousands of miles away. Sonny slowed down as they pulled into town. It appeared deserted.

"Maybe someone else has discovered something," Sonny Dille said.

"This doesn't look like a town with good news," Brian sighed.

"Let's check the motel, see if there's any messages. Ruth and Naomi must be here by now. They're probably both staying at the farm."

"It must be hard, not knowing where Jess and Ernie are." Brian was glad he was searching. The nerves jumped in his leg and he pushed it down with his hand. If he felt helpless, how on earth did Jess's mother and Ruth feel? That thought made his insides feel like he was on a fast-moving elevator going down.

The headlights of the four-by-four were reflected in puddles that stretched across the road. The sky was a dark bluish-purple with streaks of orange in the West. Tiny bats flitted between the silhouetted poplars, birch, and spruce that lined the fence by the United Farmers gas station.

Somewhere in that dark, cold bush, Jess and Ernie were sitting out the storm. Brian shuddered. He shut his eyes and willed them to be all right.

16. Jess Faces Trouble

Jess heard the thunder first, then saw a bolt of lightning crease the sky across the river towards the southwest, probably near Baptiste Lake. She decided to figure out how far away the lightning was. Grandpa Ernie had taught her and Brian how to estimate the distance one time when they'd been out camping in a storm. Sound travelled approximately a kilometer every three seconds, he had said. As the next streak of lightning crossed the sky, Jess began counting, "One thousand and one, thousand and two, thousand and three...." A mighty crash of thunder roared in her ears. The storm was getting close — about one kilometer away. The air was cold. She piled deadfall branches on the fire.

"I need help," Ernie cried. He leaned against the gnarled old tree that clung by its roots to the edge of the cliff. His good hand clutched a branch while the other feebly grasped a clump of grass. "Storm coming. Need to go home and check what's for dinner. Hope we remembered to get something out of the freezer. Don't like thunder." He continued muttering as Jess helped him stand.

"What a nice campsite you have," he continued. "Too bad I have to go home. That corned beef made a good snack, but my wife expects me for dinner, you know. Shouldn't you be going home too?"

"Your truck went off the road, Ernie. We're stuck here until someone finds us. Have another cup of tea."

"I don't want a cup of tea. People always offer me tea. What good is tea in a storm, I'd like to know?"

Another crack of thunder; the sky darkened and the cold wind blew sparks high in the trees.

" 'The heavens declare the glory of God and the firmament shows God's handiwork.' " Ernie slid to the ground in front of the lean-to. "Be a good girl, Yvonne, and get me a cup of tea, will you? I sure could use a cup of tea."

Jess had to find the hatchet or the bow saw. There was no way she could keep the fire going with twigs and deadfall. She needed more big chunks.

"Ernie, where did you hide the saw or the hatchet? It must be in the camper or truck. It's got to be."

"Ruth took them out of the camper. She said

they were dangerous. Since when are tools dangerous? First thing a human being needs — after learning how to walk, talk, and tell stories — is to learn how to use tools. We are toolmakers, tool users. On the sixth day of creation God made toolmakers. It was a good thing too."

Jess threw herself down on a damp tree stump that she was saving to put on the fire when they went to sleep. It would burn most of the night.

"That's all I need! Without tools I'll have to stay up all night tending the fire."

"Ruth took the tools, but I found them. I found the bow saw and hid it where she'd never think of it. Trouble is, I don't remember where. I don't remember much of anything these days, girl. That's a real pain. Not remembering things. It gets foggy in my head. Every once in a while ideas pop to the surface of my brain like an old log floating down the river. What is it you're looking for again?"

"A bow saw or a hatchet."

"Shouldn't go camping without them." There was a hint of accusation in Ernie's tone.

"I didn't plan it, did I?" Jess could feel her ears burning.

"Didn't you plan this trip, then?" Ernie asked. He was looking at her as if she was a stupid stranger.

Jess rose and limped up the path in the dark woods towards the debris of the camper. She was losing control, and she knew it. She leaned her head against the side of the truck cab. What was she going to do? She banged her fist on the hood.

"Try on the floor behind the truck seat," Ernie hollered. "I built a bracket for the bow saw. It's beneath the rifle."

"Why didn't you say so?" Jess screamed, as she tried to wrench open the door. "I only wanted to help. I don't know what to do, Ernie, and you've left me. Why have you left me?"

The old man looked startled at the thunder of her voice, the anger. "Why are you angry with me? You didn't tell me you wanted the bow saw. Why didn't you say something earlier, eh?"

Jess yanked on the passenger door one more time. It opened, throwing her off balance for a moment. The inside of the truck reeked of gas and damp upholstery.

First she saw the rifle. It was in its canvas carrying case. She glanced back at by the fire. She didn't like having a gun, loaded or not, near her or Ernie. She lifted it out carefully and stowed it under some of the camper wreckage where Ernie couldn't find it.

Then she returned to the truck cab and her search.

There it was — the old bow saw with its chipped red paint and two teeth missing near the top edge. Jess pulled it out.

She gazed around until she spotted a skinny birch to cut down. She needed to do this. It was better than crying or screaming at Ernie. Felling the tree wasn't too hard. It gave her a surge of confidence. She started cutting lengths for the fire. Rain spattered her hair and hands as she sawed. Sweat streamed down her forehead and into her eyes and ears, dribbled down her neck. She mopped her brow on her soaking shirt sleeve. She'd been working for ages and only had five pieces cut. When Ernie had done it, it'd looked easy. Tears of frustration mixed with the sweat.

Oh, how she wished Brian was here. Not that he'd be any better at this, but the company would be good. And sharing work would help. The fire hissed in the rain, mosquitoes dive-bombed, and a few horseflies clung to her shirt, hoping for a healthy nip.

Ernie struggled up the hill slowly. He glanced over at her, checking to find out if she was still mad at him. Jess sighed. The two of them hauled the wood down near the fire.

The old man worked beside her, piling logs and chunks of deadfall between two trees. He used his right hand, his left dangling uselessly. Maybe it was broken. It must be painful. Ernie grimaced from the effort. His face was flushed as if he had a fever.

Jess wished she hadn't screamed at him. Wished she wasn't so scared for both of them. "Sorry, Ernie."

"What have I done so wrong?" His head tilted. He shuddered. "People are so angry these days. That's why I want to go away, you know, for good. If you weren't here, I could go away. Go with the river. What is it you kids used to say — go with the flow?"

Lightning flashed nearby. A crack of thunder sounded overhead. "Quick, Ernie," Jess shouted. She helped Ernie crawl into the lean-to and pulled the car blanket over him.

"Scrunch down, sergeant, you don't want to be struck by lightning. It strikes the tallest thing handy." Ernie's thin body hit a lumpy rock under the sleeping bag and skinny mattress. "Ooph!" he complained.

"Thanks, lieutenant, you saved my skin." Jess pulled the soggy blankets over both of them. She curled up to keep her elbows and feet away from the downpour.

"I don't like the sound of bombs," Ernie said. "Never have."

Jess was going to say it was thunder, but thought better of it. If Ernie remembered something from his days in World War II, it was better than never remembering anything.

"Darned uncomfortable billet, eh sergeant?"

"It won't last long." Jess crossed her fingers, hoping. The rain pounded on the plastic, the wind howled through the trees. The river moaned as it swelled its banks. Jess peeked out. A blast of thunder shook the ground. The earth pressed hard into her ribs and knees and threatened to cut off her circulation. Her bones ached. Water from the sky filled every crack and crevice between rock and stone, clump of clay or driftwood.

"Hey, stop with the flood! Remember the rainbow!" Ernie threw off the blanket and hollered. Jess watched as the sky cleared overhead, the storm passed. Rain still hit the rushing current, bouncing and pinging, but a pale green light shone through the wet leaves on the poplar tree hanging over the river.

"It worked, Ernie, it worked. The rain's gone. The thunder's moved over to Calling Lake, I guess."

"Maybe all those years of praying have paid off, sweetheart." Ernie used his cowboy accent as he fumbled, leaning on Jess's shoulder as he pulled himself up and returned to his former spot by the tree and plopped on a sodden log. "Next time we better head for the homestead, little lady."

Thank goodness the fire had not gone out. Jess shivered in her damp jeans and T-shirt. She draped the wet blankets over one of the tent ropes. Then she crawled closer to the struggling flames.

The wind had died down and the thunder sounded further and further away. Jess toasted some buns over the spluttering fire for their bedtime snack, slathered margarine on them, and the two of them sat beside the smoke and flames and drank tea. The gentle smell of singed bread and tea circled the campfire. The birds chattered in the branches overhead, chirping their goodnights. She needed to feed Ernie and herself. Tomorrow they'd need more solid food. But what?

"Did I tell you what happened in school

yesterday?" Ernie swirled the tea in his cup. "I came upon a new kid who had left his home room to go to the washroom and got lost trying to find his way back. I had enrolled him, so I knew where he belonged. I helped him. People need to feel as if someone cares for them, you know. Otherwise they shrivel up inside. His sobs reached right into my office. I can hear him sobbing yet, inside my head. But I rescued him. He was sitting in the boys' bathroom crying his eyes out, sitting on the floor under the window. If I hadn't come along, I think he might have run away."

"A little girl in our kindergarten class got lost last week," Jess said. "The class had been playing hide and seek, down by the playground equipment. She'd climbed into one of the giant tires and fallen asleep. When she woke up she screamed. It took an hour to calm her down. Our teacher said human beings are terribly worried about being abandoned." Maybe that was more true than Jess had imagined. Didn't she feel as if Ernie was abandoning her? Her throat tightened.

Ernie's eyes drooped. "I feel like it's been one long day, little miss."

Jess took his tea mug from his right hand, and went down to the river to rinse out the mugs, rinse off the knife, and tidy up. She was still hungry. The sky overhead was dark and full of clouds again. A bunch of coyotes yapped in the distance. Only the birds and Ernie kept her company. What a lonely spot. And yet it was beautiful too. If she shut her eyes she could imagine flat bottom boats, long canoes plying the water heading towards Landis and transferring goods from boats to carts, carts to boats. This had been the route for the gold miners, the early traders, pioneer families. Now it was empty as a deserted highway.

She glanced up the hill to the clearing. The smoke from the fire sifted slowly into the sky. Ernie must be sleeping. She wasn't alone really. She had Ernie for company. She must try not to lose her temper.

The inflatable boat had fallen over and was half-filled with water. Jess turned it upside down, propped it against the tree, and tied the rope from the front to one of the branches. She stuck the two life jackets and the paddles underneath. She avoided looking at the river, but she could hear it as it rushed past.

Her mind kept whirling from one thing to another, like rapids. Food. Boat. River. Rescue. Hill. Walk. Rescue. Ernie. Fire. Rescue. Was there no end to it?

She shivered in the fading light. As she climbed up to the campsite, clutching thin willows and clumps of grass, gasping for breath, her arms and legs ached with the strain. Tired, she was so tired, and wet, and cold. Tears filled her eyes, her nose ran, her ears hurt. "Someone, please find us. I can't go on."

"Where are you? Bert, are you out there somewhere? Where's our kip, I'm hungry. Has the whole platoon disappeared?"

Jess wiped her tears away. "I'm coming, lieutenant." She handed Ernie another fruit strip. Then she lumbered up the hill and put the survival kit in the truck cab, but at the last moment she pocketed two more granola bars and the sewing kit. She closed the creaky stiff door. She pushed and strained to get two stumps on the fire, curled up under their makeshift tent and went to sleep.

17. Brian, the Investigator

Brian jammed his first piece of pizza in his mouth. The sausage nearly burnt his tongue. His father was serving himself a piece. It had been a long afternoon and evening. Now with the sky too dark to search any more they, along with several other search parties, were sitting in the Italian restaurant on Landis's main street trying to figure out what to do next. Groups of searchers had scoured the wilderness areas around each of the lakes. No one had spotted any sign of Ernie or Jess. The fear of tragedy was etched on every face. Brian ate, but the pizza tasted like cardboard.

Holly and Mark dropped by and brought them up to date. "Ruth Mather and Jess's mother are out at Ruth's brother's farm. They're sitting tight until tomorrow morning." Holly slid into the booth beside Brian.

"Yeah, we talked to them," Brian said. Actually, Sonny had talked to Naomi. She'd been crying on the phone. Brian could tell by the way his dad had spoken so soothingly, softly, saying encouraging things about how good Jess was in the bush. Brian had tried to watch the news on TV. They were talking about the search. He had flipped the switch and turned the talking heads off.

"How's it going?" Mark asked.

"It's too dark to search any more. This young man needs sleep anyway," Sonny said. "Jess and Ernie are old campers. They'll be all right."

"Not if they're hurt." Brian wiped a splash of pizza sauce from his chin. "Not with Ernie the way he is. What if a tree fell or lightning struck them?"

"Boy, are you morbid." Holly screwed up her face. "I just hope they haven't gotten separated."

"I can't figure out where they are," Brian said. "We've been to our favourite site. Other groups have checked out the rest. I don't get it. I should be able to figure out where they've gone. I found all sorts of stuff in Ernie's files. He's been a lot worse lately. He's been trying to cover up and Ruth, Jess, and her mom have been trying to protect him. They've all been lying a little. Jess didn't even want to talk to me about him." He shook his head. "That was stupid. Jess should have told me."

"You haven't been exactly sympathetic, Brian," Sonny said. "Calling him a gaga geezer got you in trouble with Jess. Most people don't want to look at the truth about themselves. Or those they love. Most people just want to go along. Let things ride," Sonny Dille said. "Getting involved is scary. It's easier to make a joke, like you do."

"It's Jess that's stupid, going with him, endangering her life. I haven't been making any jokes about that. Jess is dumb, a dumb girl." Brian could feel his ears burning, his fists clench. "Did she really think she could be a saviour? Stupid, selfish kid!"

"Really!" Holly glared at him. "Is that what you think?"

Brian paused, gripped the edge of the brown formica table in front of him, willing the touch of the cool table to calm him down. "No, she isn't—I didn't mean that. I don't know why I said it. Jess is smart about lots of stuff...social studies, language arts, science, camping and fishing and..." Brian chewed his lip, "getting along with people. Of all ages."

"You shouldn't say she's a dumb girl then!" Holly exclaimed. "I get so fed up with all the games people play. No one really cares about anyone else. It's all competition, big business, and greed."

"Easy, Holly," Mark said. "Save it for an editorial in the paper. This kid is worried."

"I'm afraid they've had an accident...." Brian pushed his plate of pizza away from him.

"When you get nervous or scared, you get

angry. You want someone to blame," Holly sighed. "Kids."

"Don't be too hard on him." Mark punched Brian's arm. "We'll find them, okay?"

Another big group of Landis Search and Rescue volunteers came through the door. Some were soaked to the skin from the wild storm that had passed. Mark's uncle and the other business people were with them. They headed for the small dining room. Mark and Holly excused themselves and followed the crowd. Brian's dad watched them leave.

"Nice kids. Holly seems pretty serious." Sonny wiped tomato from his fingers with the table napkin, refolded it, and put it back on the table.

Brian had taken all the sugar packets out of the container on the table and was putting them in order, the red sugar inscription facing up. He put them back in the white porcelain dish carefully.

"Jess wouldn't take all my jokes seriously, would she, Dad?"

"I don't know."

"I called Ernie gaga because I felt nervous. I wanted people to lighten up. Laugh."

"Jess wasn't laughing."

"I've got to find them, Dad. I've got to explain."

"Not tonight though. We'll go back to our room and check in with Ruth and Naomi once more. See how they're doing, okay?"

Brian nodded in agreement. Inside he felt miserable, worse than he could ever remember feeling.

The two of them threaded their way through the crowded room to the cashier. The older man behind the counter took their money.

"You with the search people?"

"We're friends of the family."

"Ernie Mather taught me forty years ago. He was tough but fair, you know. I learned lots, even if he was just a kid. I sure hope you find him."

"You should tell those reporters what Ernie was like. They could write a piece for the papers." Brian's dad pocketed his change and headed for the door.

"Where did you go to school?" Brian studied the man's face.

"Here."

"Here in Landis?"

"Well, not exactly. I started out in a little country school northeast of town. My parents had a farm, you know. Immigrant farmers they were, from Ukraine."

"Is that where you met Ernie?"

"I said so, didn't I, kid? He was my teacher."

"I wondered where the school was. Ernie has a hard time knowing what year it is. He might go looking for the old school."

"I don't even know if it's still there. My folks are gone, that's for sure. None of us wanted to keep the farm, you know. I went into the restaurant business, married a real Italian girl from Rome.

That's why I make good pizza, you know. Between my mother's recipes and my wife's, I can't fail."

"Don't forget to tell the young reporter all this, eh?" Brian said.

"What young reporter?"

"Mark, the young guy at the Landis Leader."

"Oh, you mean Jack's nephew?"

"He and Holly are writing articles about the whole thing."

"Holly too? I didn't know she was working at the paper. She's a real go-getter, that girl. Has a temper like her daddy though. Well, I'll be. These young people today are really somethin', you know."

"Brian, what are you doing?" His dad popped his head back in the door. "I thought you were right behind me."

"Speakin' of kids today, who are you? What's Ernie to you?"

Brian shoved open the door and hurried to the jeep. By the time he got there his dad was drumming his fingers on the dashboard. "We need to get some sleep."

"I know, I know. But I found out that guy knew Ernie years ago. We got talking." Yeah, thought Brian, the old guy was right. What was Ernie to him? Why was he up here looking for Ernie and Jess? The closer he came to the whole situation the worse he felt.

18. Ernie Awake at Night

"Starlight, star bright, first star I see tonight. I wish I may, I wish I might, have the wish I wish tonight." Ernie scanned the night sky. His young friend had gone to sleep. He listened to the crackling fire, the whispering trees, the murmuring river, and he worried.

He had come out here to do something about the growing confusion, the painful moments when his memory failed him. But this kid with him — was it someone from school or was it his own? He couldn't remember. This kid had other plans. Maybe he should trust her. She didn't seem as sad as he was. Angry sometimes, but not sad. He needed her.

He was cold, ached all over, especially his left leg and wrist, and his throat was sore. He didn't want a cold. If Ruth was here, she'd take care of him. He didn't want to go to a hospital. He didn't want to be cooped up with a bunch of old people who didn't know who they were. But he didn't want to hurt his family.

He prayed again. Rehearsing the comfortable old words chased away the nattering worries, stopped his head from whirling.

Ernie focused on the stars. He forgot the dampness, the night sounds, the hiss of the damp log in the fire, the gentle breathing of the young girl curled in her sleeping bag.

He reached out his frail right hand towards the firelight, the twinkling star. The heat from the flames warmed his fingers. He felt that warmth ripple over his cold flesh, heading towards his steadily beating heart.

God was with him. He was not alone. He did not have to face this journey by himself. He lay down and slept.

19. Night Fright

Crash! Jess woke with a start. She blinked fiercely, trying to wake her brain, figure out where she was, what had wakened her, why she was so cold and stiff. Hard ground, thin foam cushion, sleeping bag, glowing embers, river sounds. She turned her head to see Ernie sleeping, his mouth hanging open.

Bang! Crunch! Tins and glass clashing. Jess grabbed the birch staff she had peeled to poke the fire with, and leaped to her feet. It was pitch black and only a bed of coals glowed in the fire pit. She tossed a handful of kindling and a couple of branches on the embers. Sparks flew. Flames sprang to life. Her heart raced. Her muscles tightened around her bones to ward off attack. The growing light revealed dark shapes around the campfire — willow and rotting stump, dogwood and wild rosebush, and above through the trees, the bent and broken white siding of the camper, the battered truck with its door creaking. (She was sure it had been closed when she went to bed.) And someone leaning into the passenger side.

Jess gulped, froze. Her legs trembled. Something or someone was pulling stuff out of the truck cab, something dark and broad. Big. Snuffling.

"Bear!"

Her mind raced as fast as her heartbeat. Black bears are not dangerous unless they are injured, unless they are renegade, unless they are mothers with young cubs. They like camper's food. Don't go near them. Two campers were mauled in the Whitecourt forest. One boy died in Grande Prairie, attacked while he slept in his tent. Jess glanced down at Ernie, sleeping like a baby. She would not wake him. The bear had not seen her or Ernie. The bear had gone right to the truck. How had he gotten the door open? Should she lie down again and roll up in her sleeping bag? Maybe he would just eat everything in sight and go away. Then they would starve. But someone was bound to find them tomorrow. Or was it already today? Was it nearly morning or the middle of the night?

The bear was turning. He was holding her sportsbag in one paw, eating fruit strips, wrapper and all. He was glaring at her. The wind, dancing around the clearing had blown the smell of her in his direction, and then the smell of him to her.

"Yuk! You stink! Put that down, you turkey!" Jess grabbed her birch staff and the cooking pot. She walloped the side of the pot with the stick and shouted. "Go away! Go away!" The crashing reverberated in the river valley, the sounds echoed and bellowed like bulls.

The bear stood higher on his back feet, his free paw beating the air. Ernie sat bolt upright in his sleeping bag, his white hair standing out like a bush, orange in the firelight. "We're under attack, sergeant. Where's my gun?" The old man tried to pull himself up, struggled out of the lean-to, tripped over his sleeping bag, and collapsed by the fire.

Jess beat the stick on the pot and danced around the fire screaming.

The bear stood staring at the flames and Jess, and the old man, with his bedding wrapped around him, stared up at the bear. The burly animal shifted his weight and sniffed the air. The breeze blew the smell of tea, cookies, damp clothes, fire, and cold wet bodies towards the bear. He reared and snuffled.

"Don't you even think it, bozo!" Jess screamed at the top of her lungs. She reached down and grabbed a rock from the edge of the fire pit. Ouch, it was hot. She hurled the rock and it fell ten feet away from the bear and bounced.

Ernie stood slowly and joined in the barrage of shouts. He tossed a rock that banged the cab close to where the bear stood.

"Out of there. Out of there!"

The young bear squinted. He dropped to all fours and began ambling down the path towards the fire, towards their campsite. He had moved the sportsbag from his paw to his mouth. He seemed determined to hang onto it. Jess didn't have time to do more than glimpse the ridiculous picture of a burly black bear galumphing through the trees grasping the handles of a nylon black-and-fluorescent green sportsbag between his strong jaws. Jess ran, pulling Ernie with her.

Jess clasped Ernie's waist firmly. "If we follow the route the truck took, we should be able to get away." Jess struggled to keep her footing on the damp, mossy slope, tugging Ernie beside her. Her body ached as if she'd slept under a rock. Ernie wasn't a big man, but it was hard work. She knew she couldn't go far, half-carrying a hurt old man.

She didn't look back. She could hear thrashing in the woods and didn't know whether it was themselves she was hearing or the bear in pursuit. Jess tripped over a fallen log and Ernie tumbled beside her. They gasped for air. The darkness surrounded them. Jess looked behind, back down towards the fire and the river. The bear was sitting by the campfire, licking his paw. He had juice boxes and gum wrappers littering the ground around him. He was busy pulling stuff out of her sportsbag. He had forgotten all about them. The two humans shivered and wrapped their arms around each other. They didn't speak, but sat shaking, watching, catching their breath.

A fish jumped in the river. The bear cocked his head like an eager pup. He raised himself up. He looked about six feet tall and broad as a double door. With the sportsbag grasped in his teeth he ambled down, disappearing over the last ridge above the river. A series of splashes followed as he made his way along the rocky shore. He was gone.

Jess's teeth chattered. She looked over at Ernie. He was sucking on his bottom lip and the whites of his eyes looked large in the moonlight.

"It's all right now." Jess sounded more sure of herself than she felt. The two of them struggled back down the path to the warmth of the fire. Jess tucked the shivering Ernie in, checked that all the food scraps and wrappers were in the fire, tossed a couple of big hunks of driftwood on for warmth and light, and rolled up in her sleeping bag again.

She lay awake, her heart beating fast. She needed time to let it slow down. She focused on thinking about how glad she was to be alive — thinking about warm summer days and whether she'd look good with long hair and whether she should be less of a tomboy. But she liked who she was and didn't want to become a wimp and not be able to play soccer, and games with Ernie if he was well enough. How was she going to rescue him? And as she was going to sleep, she thought about the Big Bad Wolf coming for Bert and Ernie and how they ran away together. In the story Brian built his house of bricks and the two pigs ran until they came to Brian's house, where they were safe.

Where was Brian tonight, fast asleep, safe in his bed or...? Jess wondered if she would ever feel really safe again. The rising sun lit the trees on the eastern bank of the mighty river as Jess dozed off.

20. Jess Goes Fishing

Jess cast the fishing line out from shore. She cast again, the line snaking over the river, as the humming reel let the line fly. A piece of fish would taste so good. Jess couldn't remember a time when she'd ever been so hungry.

She had wakened with her stomach growling. Ernie had been sleeping beside her, his parchment skin looking damp, his forehead beaded with sweat. He did not look well. His cheeks and ears were red and hot to the touch. He had a fever. It worried her. She had slipped from the sleeping bag and headed to the river to fish. She had run a hand across the vinyl boat to see if it was still holding air. She shivered, thinking about the river, the boat, and the two of them. She hoped it wouldn't come to that.

She felt a tug on her line, reeled it in, and then let it play out. She pulled the pickerel in fast, felt him snag on a rock. The next few seconds seemed to last forever as she walked into the river, slipped on the mossy rocks, fell in with the flopping fish on her lap. She had caught their breakfast, and drenched her one set of clothes.

Jess piled the last of the driftwood and a damp stump on the fire. She cleaned and filleted the fish with Ernie watching her, making comments about her skill. She scraped the fish guts in the fire, poached the fish in a bent camp fry pan. They ate the fish and two buns each — washed down with instant coffee with coffee creamer. She wished she still had her survival kit to give them a treat, but as it was, everything tasted extra good after all the work. The campsite smelled of heat, fish, and burning logs.

Jess sat close to the fire. From her pocket, she pulled out the little sewing kit from old Mabel Teasdale and picked away with a needle at a rose thorn in her thumb. She bit her lip as she worked. Her mom would deal with this so fast, Jess wouldn't even have a chance to cry out. There, she'd pulled it out by herself. She blushed with success.

The flames danced and the heart of the fire glowed red, orange, and yellow. Even shades of blue, violet, and green appeared if Jess stared hard enough. Sparks flew into the air, the wind blew the smoke over the dark and continually moving waters. Jess draped one of the old army blankets around her. She sneezed. She'd have to dry her clothes when the sun came out and run around in underwear if the weather was warm enough. She'd tried drying Ernie's socks over the fire and burnt the toe out of one.

She had heard one plane far away and several cars and trucks going by on the road across the river behind the trees. She had seen a mother deer and her baby drinking at the water's edge. The fawn looked so fragile on its spindly legs, it had made Jess feel strong and clumsy and lucky. Lucky that she had spent so many nights camping with Ernie when he was all right, and with Brian before he turned into a clown.

"I'm glad you brought us camping with you so often, Ernie. If you hadn't, I'd be scared in the wilderness. But I'm not scared, are you?" In spite of her words, she shuddered. She was surprised by how her moods changed. She'd felt so rotten, wet, and cold coming back to the campsite with the fish; now with her tummy full, the fire so bright and warm, she felt good.

"We're safe." Ernie was chewing a broken fingernail. "When you're camping it's the little things that make you unhappy — mosquitoes, wasps, cuts, bumps. My wife is a nurse, you know. She'd help. Why isn't she here?" His thin face looked crumpled and sad. "I don't feel very good. I feel sick. I don't want to go to a hospital. I might not get out again."

Jess didn't say anything.

The black and green poplar trees, the birch and the occasional pine were silhouetted against the blue sky; a crowd of towering trees, their

144

branches whispering and waving, encircled the campfire. The knots on the green poplars looked like giant eyes staring at Jess, asking her what she was doing there; after all it was their woods not hers. The sound of the water lapping against the shoreline, the lonely song of the hermit thrush, all familiar from other camping trips, made Jess relax.

She leaned against a fat black poplar stump. She hoped her mother and Ruth weren't too worried. Surely they would know enough to trust her to take care of things. They always were after her for being super-responsible for her age. Her mother said it was because she was an only child. Ruth said she thought it was because she was someone who liked a lot of order in life. Ernie had said that it was because of her gene pool, that her grandmother had probably been like that when she was a kid. He'd taught plenty of kids like her, he said. Kids who were serious and empathic. Maybe that's why she and Ernie had been such buddies all these years. She and Brian and Ernie had always talked to each other, sung old songs, and told crazy stories. Especially by campfires. She missed that Grandpa Ernie so much.

"Tell me a story?"

"It's your turn, Bert." The old man perked up and grinned.

"Once upon a time, there were three little pigs called Bert, Ernie, and Brian. Their mother sent them out into the world to make their own way, to become independent. Bert came to a wonderful wheat field and said goodbye to the other pigs. 'I'm going to make my life right here in the sun and the wind and the beautiful prairie. I'll build my house of straw, roll in the gumbo mud, and eat grain and berries.'

"Ernie and Brian shook their heads, said their goodbyes, and went on their way. Ernie came to a grove of beautiful trees by a river. He said goodbye to Brian. 'I'm going to live here with the birds and the little furry creatures. I'll build my house of twigs and eat berries, mushrooms, and wild carrots.'

"Brian shook his head and went on his way. He came to the edge of the city where they were building a new subdivision. He spotted a vacant lot with some discarded bricks and a ruined garden. 'I will stay here. I'll be able to go to the opera and the movies, live in a fine brick house, and grow good food in my garden.'

"Then the Big Bad Wolf came calling on the three little pigs. He huffed and puffed at Bert's house and she escaped through the back door and ran lickety split to her brother Ernie's house...."

"I know how the story ends. I remember. You don't have to finish it." The sad look had gone from Ernie's face.

She had to learn to love the new Ernie somehow. Remember the old one and love the changed one. Jess threw more wood on the fire, went over and gave Ernie a little kiss on his bald spot. His skin was hot.

"Nothing like a nap after a good dinner." Ernie curled up.

"It was really Saturday morning breakfast, Ernie," Jess said quietly, and sat with her back against a deadfall poplar, staring at the flames.

21. Jess Thinks Things Through

Keep your dumb dog quiet!" Ernie shouted. A coyote howled in the distance. Jess sat up with a start, remembering where she was, rubbing her arms to get the circulation flowing. She shivered. A pale streak of light showed above the clouds in the east. It was late in the morning. Was it still Saturday?

She rubbed the sleep out of her eyes and watched as Ernie pulled himself up and wandered off in the woods a few yards to pee. He was shivering and his hair was plastered to the right side of his head. He leaned towards his good side, grasping trees as he walked. Jess would have to make him a cane out of a small birch. She sighed.

"Ernie! Don't wander off now. I'm going to build up the fire. I've got to see what the bear left us to eat. Someone will rescue us today, I'm sure of it. At least it's not winter. We could die if it was winter. But it's spring, nearly summer. We'll be all right, as long as we stick together, Ernie." While she spoke Jess was gathering dried twigs, a candy wrapper, dead grass, kneeling beside the fire pit on the cold damp ground, blowing on the glowing embers from her early morning fire, coaxing them. A small flame leapt from the bundle of twigs. She reached for broken branches and skinny sticks and fed the flame. The wonderful smell of wood smoke filled her lungs. The fire warmed her cheek. She put a couple of pieces of birch she had cut last night on either side of the fire, then laid some extra-dry deadfall poplar across the top. She stood up, brushed her sooty hands on the sides of her damp jeans, and moaned.

"I ache all over, Ernie, what about you? This isn't like camping in a nice campsite with showers and picnic shelters with roaring fireplaces, is it?" She gazed around. She couldn't see Ernie anywhere.

"Ernie? Ernie, where are you?"

The coyote howled again.

"Ernie?" Jess craned her neck to see around the trees that encircled the camp. She ran into the bush in the direction that Ernie had gone. Her heart beat like a drum. Thorns on wild rosebushes scratched her face and arms. A raven screeched, its voice harsh as a drunken bully's. "Ernie?"

She nearly tripped over him. Ernie was

propped up, leaning against a gnarled black poplar.

"I was praying," he said, and held up his still-working right hand. "Would you be so kind as to help me find my way home? I don't know how I got here, but my mother will be worried if I'm out in the woods alone. Call my brother Pete, he'll come and get me. I prayed and you came."

Jess gulped mouthfuls of fresh morning air. For a moment she had been worried sick, worried she had lost Ernie. Holding his too-warm body close to her, walking with him back to their camp, she started to cry.

"Don't wander off like that, Ernie," she shouted. "You scared me. You could get lost."

"I am lost, that's the problem." Ernie yanked his hand from hers and struggled ahead on his own, grasping tree trunks and dogwood bushes to keep himself upright.

He slumped onto one of the huge stumps close to the fire and put his head on his right hand. His face was red and blotchy. His left leg stretched out at an odd angle. His clothes were covered with dirt and leaves. His shoes were untied. His golf jacket had a streak of grass stain and one of oil. He shuddered, pulled his right arm and shoulder up and in as if to keep his bones warm. He looked sick.

Jess had a sudden flash of memory of one time years ago when she and Brian and Ernie had gone fishing at Baptiste Lake. Brian had caught a pike, and she had caught nothing. When they had pulled the boat in to land for lunch and a potty break, she, little Jess, had been angry, angry that Brian had caught fish and she hadn't, so she'd run off in the bushes pouting, half a baloney sandwich in her hand. She remembered the sharp smell of mustard, even glanced down to see if the streak of yellow was still on her hand. She had been frightened. She'd called and called until her voice was hoarse. Finally, after what felt like hours, Ernie and Brian had found her, hugged her, and Ernie had carried her back to the boat on his strong shoulders.

Jess moved towards the campfire and picked up the coffee pot with the rolled sleeve of Ruth's sweater. The least she could do was to carry Ernie now. He didn't need someone being mad at him.

"Have we been abandoned here?" Ernie gazed into her eyes as she handed him a cup of instant coffee.

"No, we haven't," she said calmly. Jess tested the coffee with her lip. It was too hot to drink yet, so she wrapped her two hands around the cup for warmth, and the safety of holding something familiar.

"I have to go for help, Ernie." She felt his forehead. The old man's fever was getting worse.

"I don't like being alone, do I?"

"I could get food. Aren't you hungry?" The situation was worse than she thought. "Do you feel all right?"

But Ernie had stopped listening. He was

staring into the flames and humming a hymn. Jess picked up one of the blankets and wrapped it around his shoulders. Then she slid down to the beach and searched for any packets of treats or juice cartons that might have been missed by the bear. She found one apple juice and a granola bar lying by a rock. She had the last two granola bars stored in her back pocket for emergencies. She spotted her Swiss Army knife in the shallows of the river. She thought her hand would freeze reaching for it. The pebbles and rocks under the current jostled and bumped as she grabbed the knife. She scoured the beach and cove for more items, with no luck. The river gurgled and hummed. It was a silty greenish-brown wide river, with the occasional branch or log cruising by at quite a speed. Maybe with a good boat, she thought, but not a silly inflatable. She pushed the scary proposition away. Ernie wouldn't be able to row. It would be just her and the river.

Except for a circling hawk, a flutter of wings on the far bank, she and Ernie were in the wilderness alone. Jess gulped and her ears popped. The sky above was filled with large, heavy, fast-moving clouds. They looked menacing. With the chill wind coming down the river, blowing into her face, she'd say another storm was coming their way. One of those late spring snowstorms that kill all the fresh green leaves, tender plants, early blossoms. A mosquito bit her cheek.

"You're in for a surprise, you pest, the winter

isn't over yet." She rubbed the sting. The back of her hand was covered with a pattern of thorn scratches, one knuckle red and raw from sawing. Her feet squished in the soggy sneakers, her jeans felt clammy and cold, and her body craved a hot bubble bath. "Mom would be shocked at how ready I am for a nice long soak in the tub," she told the flowing water.

"Have you gone?" Ernie's anxious voice called.

"Not yet. I was trying to find anything left by the bear. He took my sportsbag." Jess scrambled up the steep bank to the campsite. Her stomach rumbled. She wanted a banana and a glass of orange juice so badly she could taste them. Her mom always had fresh bananas in a bowl in the middle of the dining room table. She blinked, thinking about her mom and Ruth, worrying themselves sick.

By now with any luck they were staying at Grandma Ruth's relatives. When Jess's dad had moved out, Ruth had brought Naomi and Jess to the farm for a few days. Ruth's brother said the two women were like the Bible story about Ruth and Naomi, except in the Bible Naomi had been the mother and Ruth the younger woman. The point of the story was that Ruth and Naomi journeyed together and made a home for themselves. Jess was glad her mom and Ruth had done that — stayed together ever since she, Jess, had been little. She loved them both.

She sighed and thought of the long climb up past the truck cab, up the ridge to the next flat area, and finally up the last ridge to road level. She would have to walk along the gravel road until she came to a farm. How far was it? How she wished she had company for that journey.

There would be search teams looking for them. Last year a girl and her dog had wandered away from a campsite near Red Deer and been found after three days, safe. Jess held on to that encouraging story.

Jess gave Ernie her birch staff, the juice pack, and the granola bar. She took her Swiss Army knife and cut a sapling for a walking stick, giving it a sharp tip. She took the compass out of her pocket and checked due north. She was going to walk east up the hill. It was important not to get lost. She loaded the fire with fresh logs, hunted through the debris of the camper for anything besides Grandma Ruth's big sweater to put on over her wet clothes. She found spare bug repellent for Ernie. A tin of beans rolled out as she shifted the cabinet. Mentally she thanked the universe for lunch.

"I'm going now, Ernie. It may take a while. I'm going for help and food."

Ernie looked up, a puzzled expression on his face.

"Don't leave the fire, okay? You tend the fire."

He stared into the flames. "Mend the tire, right."

Jess shook her head. She looked up at the sky. A cloudy afternoon. She'd have to hurry.

Jess rolled up the sleeves of the big sweater, double-knotted her sneaker laces, and picked up the freshly peeled staff.

"Well, I'm off to see the world, Ernie." The words floated in the air like smoke.

The path that the truck had slashed through the woods was clear. Jess followed it up the steep bank towards the road. She had to grasp at shoots and willows to pull herself up. She must have half a kilometer or so of rough terrain to cover. She didn't know how far it was to civilization. Coyotes didn't bother people, did they? The bear was long gone, wasn't he? Ernie wouldn't wander away again, would he? Would she find help soon enough?

The sky above darkened. Wind in the treetops moaned. A loud crash, a feeling of the ground shifting beneath her, told her a tree had fallen in the forest. A squirrel scolded from a spruce grove. Jess collapsed under a giant pine tree. The ground was littered with pine cone shells, husks, and tiny mushrooms. It smelt of rich earth and musty leaves. Jess picked some Labrador tea and put it in her pocket. She was afraid of eating the mushrooms. She only knew two varieties for sure — green rusellas and boletas with their bright orange tops and hairy stems.

She could see the trees silhouetted against the sky by the top of the first ridge. Another ten minutes and she should be at the road.

"If it wasn't for Ernie teaching me about the woods, fishing, camping, and life outdoors, I'd be in a real pickle," she told the squirrel who was chattering away from a branch of the tree. It must be awful for poor Ernie, who knew all sorts of stuff, to lose his memory. A writer who had visited Jess's class last year had reminded them that creativity in art and stories came from memory and imagination.

"I'm building memories and Ernie's losing them. What a pair!" She gripped a dogwood branch and continued her journey up the steep bank. Her foot slipped. Her hand stung like blazes where she grasped a thorny rosebush instead of a dogwood. She would have to get the needle out again when she came back. A bee buzzed close by. A plane droned overhead. The smell of rotting wood assailed her as she climbed. Gashed topsoil with grubs and beetles crawling in among turned-up roots, smashed saplings, and torn leaves and blossoms revealed the path of the truck. A cloud of midges circled her head. She swatted them and looked down towards the campsite near the beach.

Smoke and sparks rose from the fire, all she could see of the campsite through the foliage of early spring. She had come further than she thought.

Jess stood stock still on the hill, a few hundred meters from the top. Her heart beat fast and she gasped for breath. Down below was Ernie by the campfire, hopefully putting a log on now and then.

"Help! Help! Fire!" Ernie's voice rang out.

Jess sprang down the slope as if the bear were after her, leaping and diving, sliding and slipping, past the spruce grove, the chattering squirrel, the bank of dogwoods. She stumbled down the steep bank. A poplar tree that she didn't remember lay in her path. She boosted herself up and as she did, she heard a loud crack. The log beneath her shifted and crashed to the forest floor. Her left foot was caught under a branch. A long scrape with drops of blood spurting from it appeared on her ankle. She wiggled and wiggled until her foot came free, leaving her sneaker trapped. The pain in her foot and ankle was severe. She had to get the sneaker. She pulled with all her might. Finally the shoe dislodged.

Far below near the water black smoke rose in the air.

Jess hobbled down the hill, not putting weight on her left foot, grimacing in pain.

"Help! Help! Bert, where are you?"

"I'm coming," she hollered. Her voice sounded like a screech. Her foot hurt so badly she wanted to cry.

Ernie stood by the truck, his right hand holding the jack, his white hair flying in the cold wind. The tire had rolled down the slope into the campfire and was engulfed in flames. It smelled horrible. Jess grabbed Ernie's old work gloves and the birch fire stick and rolled the tire down the hill and into the river. It sizzled and spat. Then she grabbed Ernie's arms and hollered. "What were you trying to do?"

"You said mend the tire. I remember that." He grinned. Ernie stared at the jack in his hand, the wrench and nuts from the back wheel of the truck lying on an oily rag on the ground. He shrugged his shoulders. Jess couldn't figure out how he had managed to take the tire off with only one working hand.

"How can I help, Ernie? I don't know what to do." Jess cried. Her foot hurt. "Sometimes you're all right. Sometimes you aren't." She threw herself down. "I shouldn't get so mad. It's not your fault." Jess wiped the tears from her eyes. How did her mom care for so many people? Naomi never lost her temper with them. She never even got angry with Jess. I want my mom, she thought. I want to see her so bad my insides hurt as bad as my outsides.

Ernie shook his head, and blinked.

"At least, you're safe. That's what's important." Jess rocked back and forth. The pain in her ankle made her teeth ache.

"Am I safe?" Ernie stared at her, his eyes dark and sad. "Am I really?"

22. Brian Finds a Clue

Brian and his dad were driving down the back road toward Ernie's old school. They'd stopped and gotten directions from the restaurant owner. Sonny had slept in, much to Brian's dismay. It was early afternoon Saturday and they'd had a late pancake brunch out at Grandma Ruth's brother's farm. The RCMP wanted Ruth to stay put. Naomi didn't want to leave Ruth, but at the same time she wanted to join the search. Sonny and Brian had said they would meet them in town later and check signals.

"Doing nothing is harder than you can imagine," Naomi had told Brian.

"We'll phone if we find anything," Sonny had promised.

As they turned down the side road that led to the school, the smell of something nasty burning wafted in the air. A strong wind was blowing from the north.

"What's that?" Sonny asked. He peered through the window as if the gravel road ahead would give him an answer.

"Probably from the pulp mill, or natural gas," Brian said. "There's always something stinking up here. I wish they'd leave the earth alone, instead of prodding it, digging it up, tossing trees down."

"It's the old environment versus economy battle. A developer bought my father's farm in Trinidad for peanuts, cut it up, and sold it for thousands. Nearly killed the old man. He couldn't take it. Started drinking. No wonder I don't like the country. It kills people."

"It doesn't have to, Dad. You have to learn to live with it — not let it overwhelm you. Some people treat nature as if it were the enemy. Cooperation is the key." Brian flipped through the cassette tapes looking for some cool tunes. "That's what Ernie used to say."

"Ernie gave you a lot of good advice."

Brian nodded. Please, Ernie, don't be dead, not before I see you. He wanted to say thanks.

"Is that the cemetery the RCMP said to watch for?" Brian tossed the cassettes aside. "The school is supposed to be in the next woods." An overgrown arch of caragana bushes fronted a small field surrounded with white poplar and silver birch. The car slowed.

"I see it! I see it!" Brian pointed to a dilapidated log building with a row of windows with tiny panes in them. The car pulled off the freshly gravelled road onto a grass track. The grass was beaten down by tires from trucks and four-by-fours.

"Maybe that's their tracks," Brian said hopefully. "Maybe they're here."

His dad patted Brian's shoulder as the two of them walked to the old school. "I never noticed what a stubborn guy you are, Brian. When you decide to do something, watch out."

The schoolhouse was empty, except for two old desks and rows upon rows of stored mushrooms that some squirrel family had forgotten. The teacherage was no bigger than an old-fashioned one-car garage and held a broken bedspring and one end of a metal bed. A different family of small animals had lined all the shelves with mushrooms.

"Life moves on. What we don't use, some other critter does," Sonny Dille said. "I'm beginning to understand old Ernie Mather."

"I was hoping they'd be here," Brian sighed. He led the way out the door and around the back. A dinted, ancient tackle box lay open, rusting in the grass. "I wonder if that was Ernie's?"

Brian's dad had gone striding down a grass track towards the river. Brian ran to catch up with him.

"Spooky, isn't it?" Brian said.

His dad kept walking. "Is that how it feels to you, spooky?"

Brian took giant steps to keep up with his

dad, glad he was finally big enough to keep up. "I guess it just feels like a lot of people, real people, went to that school, and walked through these fields just like us. It's as if...."

"Opening the door to this old schoolhouse we see the whole history of human beings in this country," his dad mused, "complete with mouse droppings, chipmunk nests, and mushroom stores. I envy Ernie in some ways. He at least knew enough to remember his roots and return to them." Sonny Dille bent over and pulled on a stalk of grass until the fresh sprout slid out. He stuck the tasty new growth into his mouth.

Brian reached over and took his father's big hand in his for a moment and the two of them strode towards the river. He could hear the swish and gurgle of the current over rocks on the other side of the rise.

The rushing river showed through the trees. Dark, full clouds skimmed the hills on the other side. The smell of something stinky, like burning rubber, was worse here.

"I wish I knew they were all right," Brian sighed as they skittered down the bank to the pebbly beach that stretched out into the river. A startled deer launched into the current and swam over to an island in the centre. The end of the island was stacked with weathered logs, stumps, and branches thrown up by high water or storm. "I feel like they've been lost for days. But it's only been twenty-four hours."

The two of them wandered along the water's

edge looking for clues of some recent fire or visit.

Brian's dad wiped his forehead with his new red cowboy handkerchief. He sat on a bleached pine log with roots taller than a bear. "I don't think they've been here."

"When we find them, I want to talk to Jess. I need to explain...."

"That you're a normal kid. That you make mistakes. What?"

Brian pointed to some blackish smoke upstream. He was ignoring his dad's remarks. He didn't know what he was going to say to Jess. If she'd talk to him.

He was standing at the river's edge, watching the deer scramble out of the water and disappear on a path into some birch woods on the narrow island. "What's that funny thing hooked onto that driftwood?"

Man and boy shielding their eyes, they focused on the back of the island where the pile of driftwood balanced like a giant game of pick-up sticks. Sure enough, there was some hunk of lime-green neon fabric caught on one of the logs.

"It's a funny place to leave your bathing suit," Dad laughed.

"Doesn't look like a swimsuit. Looks like a backpack or something." Brian scratched the top of his head, squinted, tried to see what the thing was. It puzzled him. A roll of thunder echoed in the distance. The cold front that made a whole line of clouds across the sky blocked out the last vestige of the sun.

"I think it's time we went to town, met Ruth and Naomi, and caught up on the progress of the others. There's nothing more we can do here. I don't like the look of that sky." Brian's dad led the way to the four-by-four.

"We just got here," Brian protested.

He kept dragging his feet, staring over his shoulder, back towards the river and the shrinking view of the island with its splash of colour draped on the bleached and battered logs. He shivered. He tiptoed around the schoolhouse, not wanting to disturb its ghosts, and stared up at the tall spruce by the front door. Then he walked slowly towards the car. Something bright and out of place caught his eye. It was orange and wet from rain, looked like it had fallen off a low willow branch. Brian picked the soggy wool thing up.

"It's one of Jess's flashy cool-down socks, Dad," Brian shouted. "She's been here."

Sonny Dille hurried back to the spot where Brian was standing, holding the soggy sock.

Brian stared around, swept the landscape with his eyes. He could see no other signs of human life. "Finally, a clue. But where did they go from here? Where's the truck? Where are Jess and Ernie?" Brian squeezed his eyes shut, trying to block the scary thoughts that leapt into his mind.

"We've got to go back to town!" Brian shouted. "Report what we've seen."

"We need a full-fledged search out here."

Brian's dad ran to the car and grabbed his car phone. "Give me the RCMP please. We've got some information."

"Why, oh, why did she go with him?" Naomi sat beside Brian in the café of the Landis Hotel. Sonny and Ruth sat across from them. She was folding and unfolding the damp and grimy orange sock, staring at it as if it might give her some answers. A TV crew was having mid-afternoon coffee across the room. A group of Venturers, Scouts, and Junior Forest Rangers was getting briefed in the lobby.

The cellular phone was lying on the centre of the table. Not one of the family and friends looked like they had slept for days, even though it had only been yesterday morning when Ernie had taken the truck.

"I would have done the same thing," Brian said. "If I had seen Ernie leaving in the truck. We know he's not supposed to drive."

"But why didn't she get help?" Naomi's high-pitched voice had developed a raspy quality. Black circles ringed her eyes. She shoved the sock into her large purse. Then Naomi began picking at her french fries, shoving them around the plate, tracing patterns in the ketchup, not eating them. "I would have come home. I could have stopped him."

Ruth took Naomi's hand in hers. The old woman's hands were shaking, like the trembling aspens by the schoolhouse, Brian thought.

"It's not your fault," Ruth said. "I was the one who left the house, thinking Ernie was asleep. You and I thought we had hidden the keys well enough. Both of us have been trying to protect Jess and Ernie. It didn't work. The important thing is to find them now. I feel so useless. I want to go looking. I can't stand doing nothing. I know the RCMP think it's better to have the family stay in one place — in case Ernie comes to his senses and tries to contact me — but staying at my brother's house has been really difficult. He and his wife and their kids all look like it's a funeral. I can't give up hope. It's not my style."

"They both know the woods. I don't think Ernie has forgotten that yet." Naomi pushed away her plate. "I'm with you, Ruth, I don't want to sit and wait any longer. I want to go looking. Especially now that Brian has found out where they've been."

The waitress brought a fresh round of coffee. Brian ordered another soft drink. Some part of the puzzle was out of place. He couldn't analyze what it was. That must be the way Ernie felt all the time, like someone had mixed everything up while he wasn't looking.

The phone on the table rang. Sonny picked it up. It was Mark Saunders.

"They're calling the searchers, telling them to take shelter. There's another storm on its way. Holly and I are taking a TV crew out to the old schoolhouse to show them where Ernie taught, show them the river where he used to fish."

Brian's dad relayed the whole message word for word.

"Wait a minute!" Brian shouted. "What colour was Jess's sportsbag? Neon green and black, right?" He banged his forehead with the flat of his hand. Stupid!

The whole of his insides knotted into one mass of fear. Jess's sportsbag caught on a piece of driftwood in the middle of a roaring river. Her sock dropped by the schoolhouse. Where was Jess? She never went anywhere without that heavy bag. In the wilderness it really would be a survival kit, and she'd be lost without it. Lost or drowned. He didn't dare say what he thought out loud. As it was, Grandma Ruth and Naomi were staring at him.

"Brian, you look like you've seen a ghost. Are you all right?" Ruth put her hand on his arm. "What about Jess's sportsbag?"

"Nothing, it's nothing," Brian pulled away, afraid for all of them. "We should go back to the schoolhouse though. They've got to be out there, somewhere close by. I feel it in my bones." Brian willed Jess and Ernie to be all right.

Ruth sighed. "Ernie and I danced the polka at the community dance in that school over fifty years ago. We danced up a storm."

"Too bad we couldn't dance away this storm. Jess and Ernie are out in it somewhere," Naomi groaned. "We'll go with you, if that's all right, Sonny. Sitting around gives me a headache."

Ruth and Naomi went to the washroom before

paying the bill. Brian ran for the car. His dad caught up to him.

"What's up, Brian?"

"No way would Jess Baines be separated from her sportsbag, and that was her sportsbag caught on the driftwood in the middle of the Athabasca River, I'm sure of it."

"How would it get out there in the middle of the river?" Sonny asked.

"Am I awfulizing, Dad? I'm afraid they might have drowned." Brian's head throbbed.

"Always think of three options, Brian." Sonny polished the mirror on the passenger side of the car three times as he talked. Brian knew he was trying to calm him down. Maybe he was trying to calm himself, Sonny, down too. "Don't move to the negative so fast. She could have lost the sportsbag. It could have fallen in the river."

"I don't want to tell Naomi or Ruth," Brian whispered as the two women came out of the café. "I usually blurt everything out first thing. I don't want to do that. Not this time." Suddenly he remembered himself and Ernie and Jess out in the middle of Baptiste Lake. Brian had dropped his fishing pole overboard. Seeing as it was a bright August day, Ernie had dived in to rescue it. "We'll not tell the wimmen folk, eh?" he'd said. "They wouldn't approve of me swimming out here with no other grownups around. No need to worry them with silly stuff." Brian's eyes smarted with hot tears. Please, let Jess and Ernie be all right.

23. Jess Makes a Tough Decision

Jess and Ernie huddled on the beach in the shelter of the small cliff. It was the middle of Saturday afternoon. She and Ernie had eaten the tin of beans for lunch, but there hadn't been any buns left. Now she was hungry again.

The rain had started as a fine drizzle. Wind blew the tops of the trees back and forth like palm fronds in a breeze. The air had turned cold, the sky dark. Thunder echoed across the river. Jess watched the river, the rain pouncing, bouncing on its surface. The ancient, dark, and mysterious river. It loomed before her, filling the landscape. She felt as if it surged through her, tumbled her like a rock. Now it was the rain's turn to do that.

"The rain will put out the fire." Ernie said. "Reminds me of the time we camped out in the rain all one weekend, never caught a fish, only caught a cold."

"That wasn't me."

"Pete and I camped out. Pete's a good camper. You'd like my brother Pete. He'll come, Pete will."

"I'd welcome anyone right now," Jess sighed. "I've lost my bag to the bear, twisted my ankle under a log, and now it's swollen and hurts like blazes. I'm cold and hungry and it's raining." Jess turned her face away so Ernie couldn't see the tears streaking her grubby face. The view downriver through her wet lashes was depressing. Brown waves swirled, a deep mist filled the valley, driving rain pelted the racing torrent. The rain bounced on the river like pennies on cement, a million splashes per second. Whitecaps formed on the glacier-fed river.

Suddenly the rain turned to white pellets pinging and banging on the ground, bouncing on the surface of everything, smashing tender leaves and shoots. Fresh spring growth fell and early rose petals were beaten to shreds by the hail. Piles of hailstones as big as peas mounded at the bases of trees. The crash of a giant elm made the ground beneath Jess shake. The tops of the skinny poplars bent and twirled like maniacal dancers. The air filled with violent sounds of cracking branches, falling trees, smashing waves. This was no ordinary storm. It was chaos. Ernie and Jess shivered under their soaking blankets, hid their faces on their bent knees to keep the hail away. A tree on the other side of the river twisted like a licorice swirl and plopped into the river. Rocks fell from the cliff and then disappeared in the raging current.

"Stop this infernal racket!" Ernie shouted into the wind. He coughed and spluttered. He flung his head up. His face was covered with rain and dirt. His eyes flashed in anger. "It's enough I can't remember where I am. I don't need the devil turning my universe into a disaster area."

Jess's teeth chattered. It was a cinch the search parties wouldn't be out in this. Sitting here at the bottom of a steep river valley, beside a crazy river that used to be a highway to everywhere and now was a wilderness wracked by storm, Jess felt trapped. Ernie had folded his hands. His red-rimmed eyes had a faraway look. His nose was running. He coughed.

Time was running out. They had no food. Ernie was sick. He could die of pneumonia. She had come with Ernie, she was responsible for him. Her job was to keep him safe. She didn't have the security blanket of her bag, she didn't have the use of her feet, what with the swollen ankle. She did have the use of her brain. She would have to think her way out of this.

She leaned across and stroked Ernie's arm. The tears that ran down her cheeks now, mingling with the cold rain as the storm passed, were tears of sorrow, tears for Ernie and for herself. It was one thing not having the security of familiar things like her bag, it was something else not having the physical strength to use all your limbs. She shook her head to forget the pain of the foot. It must be worse for Ernie, losing the ability to think, to recognize the familiar. What would it be like to lose your memories in a fog? Would it be like having everything you knew or remembered bob to the surface like so many broken branches on a wide river and then disappear around the next curve? It would be better to die, or to cross the bridge to the world of the really sick who didn't remember that they didn't remember, to the land of the truly unconscious like Mabel Teasdale.

While she sat there shivering, hugging her knees, staring at the river rolling by, the storm passed as fast as it had come. The sky to the north cleared. The old man mopped his face with a wet sleeve. She and Ernie had weathered a second big blow and come through. Knowing Alberta, there would be another one tomorrow. She had had enough. She had to make a move.

Jess looked around her, up the hill towards their campsite. The fire was dead out, a big puddle formed around some black charred logs. The lean-to had collapsed. The truck was a forlorn hulk.

"I want to go home," Ernie said emphatically. "I'm hungry."

"Me too," Jess pulled herself up by her good side. She grabbed the walking stick she had peeled with her Swiss Army knife and forced herself to walk, picking a path through the rocks, mud, and thick grasses to where she had stored the boat. She leaned on the black poplar tree, held on to its rough wet bark as a support, untied and lowered the boat. It took her ages. Everything she did took twice as long as she thought it should. Her foot ached.

"I've decided we can't wait to be rescued, Ernie," she said out loud, even though she was pretty sure he couldn't hear her, didn't know who she was right now. She talked to him anyway. "As soon as the river calms down a bit and we're sure the storm has really gone for good, we'll float down to Landis." Saying it out loud would mean she had to do this. She glared at the river as if it were a bully she had to put in its place. Her nightmare rose in her imagination like a ghost in a haunted house. A chill ran along her backbone.

She rubbed her forehead with her hand. Her brow was damp. Ernie's face was flushed. Another day out here could be dangerous for him...she didn't dare say the real word, "fatal." She was struggling in her mind with several problems. Old Ernie would have said, "If you get lost, stay put. Don't move. Let searchers find you. Light a fire." Old Ernie would have worried about the river after a storm, the strength of the boat, the speed of the current, the length of the journey.

Did she have any other options? She couldn't walk out, not with this ankle. She was afraid staying put would be too hard on Ernie. They had no food or dry clothes. Even the option of lighting a large signal fire was a foolish hope with the wet wood and her sore foot and damaged knee. The steady pain made her feel sick to her stomach. No, her only real chance was the river.

The river, the eternal rushing river. She didn't know whether to trust the two of them to it or not. If only Ernie could help her make up her mind. But he was too sick.

She was scared — scared to go, scared to stay. It could go badly either way. Her mom called it being caught between a rock and a hard place.

She spoke out loud to Ernie again. "The searchers are probably looking at the lakes where you used to fish. They wouldn't think of the river. If what you said is right, this should take us floating back to town before nightfall, to the town dock, or the camping spot by the river where we sometimes parked. We could sleep in a real bed tonight."

Her foot throbbed. She chewed the corner of her lip as she hauled the boat to the edge of the river. She shivered from cold and her stomach rumbled. She licked drops of water off her chin. She really should give Ernie a drink. He could get dehydrated. She scooped up river water with a tin cup from the old camping set and took it to him. "I don't think one cup of river water will hurt you."

He held the cup in both hands and slurped like a baby. "Thank you very much, young lady." Jess pulled her comb out of her pocket and combed the silky white hair away from his eyes, zipped the soggy golf jacket up as if it would protect him.

She pulled the last two granola bars out of her back pocket. They were damp and flattened. She unwrapped them with a little flourish, sat down beside Ernie and passed him one. "Here, this may be the last bit of food for quite a while," she said softly. Thank goodness for those beans she'd found, heated in the frying pan for lunch a couple of hours ago. She needed the strength food energy would give her for paddling.

They sat in silence munching, while Jess waited for the last of the wind to die down, waited for the courage to do what had to be done.

She closed her eyes and hoped she'd made the right decision. She had to trust the boat and the river to carry them to safety, to carry them home.

"Ernie, you'll have to help put the boat in the water. I can't do it alone." Jess handed him the cane. She limped to the edge of the river, wading into the water, tugging the boat beside her, turned to see Ernie eyeing the river and the boat suspiciously. He was such a small man, looked like a strong wind would blow him over. What if they didn't make it?

She strained to keep the boat parallel with the shore long enough to coax Ernie into the front.

"My brother Pete and I entered the annual canoe race from Mirror Lake to Landis one year. We had a good sturdy canoe, not like this. This isn't a canoe," Ernie said, as he tried to climb into the front of the boat without either falling or capsizing the craft. He dropped the cane. Jess leaned on her good leg and supported him as he dropped into the boat. She pulled him up by his thin shoulders so he was sitting upright. Ernie kept talking about the canoe race, as if the words he spoke were easing his worry, as if this scrap of memory was a protection against the fear that hovered over the two of them. "That was before Pete went away. We didn't win, but we had a great time. Is this a race?"

Jess nodded her head as she fell into the back of the boat with a groan. She pushed off from the rocky shore, glancing longingly at the solid shore, the rocky beach, the sandy cliff, and the wild and lonely woods above. The boat had begun to move into the current, away from their tiny beach.

What a strange journey. They'd always used this boat on calm lakes. Never on a rushing river. It was like sitting on a sponge. The vinyl sides folded around them, the water raced beneath them. What if they capsized? She should have put on a life jacket. What a dumb kid. She hauled the two life jackets she'd collapsed onto out from under her bottom, passed one to Ernie. He tried to drop it over his head with his good right hand. Every move either of them made rocked the boat, but somehow Jess got the jackets on. She remembered a roller coaster ride when her stomach lurched and her heart raced like this.

A blue heron took off smoothly as they moved with the current down the east bank of the river. Oh, how she envied him his wings.

Jess paddled just enough to get them into the fastest part of the current and keep them away from the rocks. Floating logs worried her. The storm was over, but debris had fallen in the river. Trees lined the banks, a steep, sheer cliff appeared on the east side. Jess's heart skipped a beat thinking about what would have happened if the truck had gone over the edge there instead of where it did. Up ahead small islands dotted the middle of the river. Jess handed Ernie the tin cup, "Bail, will you, Ernie. Water's getting into the boat."

"Fast water!" The old man was leaning to one side of the boat, leaning on his good side, trailing the cup in the water like a kid with a stick. He was grinning, too. "My mother read Pete and me *The Wind in the Willows*. Remember when Rat took Mole out for the first time in a boat and they had an upset? I remember that as if it had happened to me. I like stories."

"I've too much work to do."

"That's what my mother used to say."

"Ernie, can't you see what we're doing here?"

"We're going down the river, just like Rat and Mole. Telling stories will pass the time."

"One of my favourites was Winnie-the-Pooh." Jess pulled her mind away from the fear and tried to think about a story for Ernie, wished she was a kid again, a little kid curled up on her mother's lap, listening. "I like all of the stories. But my favourite is the one where Pooh got stuck in Rabbit's front door after eating all of Rabbit's honey. He asked Christopher Robin to read him a book because he was a bear in great tightness."

"We're in great tightness, right?" Ernie sighed. He started to bail. 'When you walk through a storm' — I wish I could remember the rest of it. Songs help."

Jess felt a bump as the boat slid across a high rock. She clutched the sides in sheer panic as a log hurtled past. They were being swept along in the current and Jess had very little control over the boat. It went where it willed. She scanned the empty river, the silent sky, the deserted banks, and cried out.

"Ernie, I'm afraid."

24. Brian Leads the Way

When Brian and his dad burst into the Landis Leader office, Mark and Holly stood over the table with the ordinance map spread out in front of them. Pins and tags marked where search and rescue teams were located. Two camera operators and a news-woman were helping themselves to coffee. The TV truck was parked out front. Holly paced the floor.

"The teams have covered the lakes and searched all the small cabins, summer homes, back roads. There is no sign of the camper or Jess and Ernie. I don't understand it," Holly sighed, gesturing with her arms spread wide. "We've had crazy phone calls from Revelstoke, British Columbia, Billings, Montana, and Swift Current, Saskatchewan, with sightings. I'm amazed how many people care about this. It's like everyone wants to help." She shook her head in surprise. "The RCMP are stumped. So are we. Without more clues we're searching for a needle in a haystack. Even Mighty Mark is getting worried...."

"That's why we're here," Brian interrupted. "It's a clue."

"We're going back to the pioneer school," Sonny Dille said. "Brian thinks that Jess's sportsbag is hanging on a piece of driftwood in the middle of the river. They could have gone over a cliff, they could be hurt, or worse still, they may have drowned in the river."

"Grandma Ruth and Naomi are waiting in the car. We haven't told them what we're afraid has happened. We just told them about the cool-down sock. They've got enough fears of their own." Brian ran his hand through his curly hair. So do I, he thought, so do I.

"I'm going for my dad's jet boat." Holly nearly knocked the table over dashing for the door.

The TV crew glanced up at the raised voices. The newswoman ran over.

"What's up? I thought we were going to the pioneer school, Mark."

"We are. We're going to follow these guys. Unless you want to go in the jet boat. Brian saw something...." The TV people clustered around Mark.

Brian didn't wait to hear. He had to get back to the school, and fast.

He and his dad clambered into the four-by-four with Ruth and Naomi. Just past the bridge close to the golf course, Brian spotted a funny looking surveyor's ribbon. "That's not a surveyor's marker. That's Jess's other gym sock."

"So," Naomi said slowly, "Jess left these socks as markers. She must have thrown this one out as they passed this way. Then the one at the old schoolhouse. But where did they go from there?" Sonny stopped beside the willow trees and Brian ran over and rescued the sock. He handed it to Naomi. It was soggy from all the rain. She put it into the plastic bag she had the other sock in.

"If anything has happened to Jess, I'll never forgive myself!" Ruth peered out the window as the truck spat gravel, rushing down the side road. "I should have kept a closer watch on Ernie." Brian glanced back at Ruth. Her usually cheerful face looked thin and drawn. She seemed to have aged in the last two days.

Naomi sat with her knees tight together, her hands clasped in her lap, her knuckles white. The two women swayed with the bumps in the speeding four-by-four.

"I can't believe I missed seeing that marker the first time. I must have been blind." Brian set his face grimly to the front, watching for the cemetery, the grove of trees, and the old school. He had to take another look at what was clinging to the driftwood. He hoped it was not Jess's ugly overstuffed "survival kit."

As they turned into the grassy lane that led to the schoolhouse, Brian let out a moan. A huge branch had fallen, smashing the roof of the school. Splinters of glass and shutters lay everywhere. The car edged past the building and wound its way down towards the steep track. An impassable stretch of driftwood blocked their way. The four of them jumped out, climbed over the driftwood, and raced down the slope towards the water's edge. The stones were slippery. Ruth and Naomi held each other's hands and made their way to the shore.

"This is where Ernie used to fish when he taught in that school." Ruth asked, "Could he have come back here? After all this time?"

Naomi was clutching the plastic bag with the orange socks in her hand, as if they could give her more answers. She was scanning the beach, the opposite shoreline, the woods to the north. "We should be able to spot a campfire."

"Not after the last storm." Brian said.

Brian and his dad stared across at the island, hands shielding their eyes. The shape of the island had changed. A huge raft of logs had come unstuck from the back of the island and was moving downstream.

"It's gone." Brian waded out into the rushing current, let the cold silty water push against his legs. He shivered as the force of the current, the chill from the glacial stream, attacked him. He felt defeated, scared. "It's gone."

"Come back, son!" Brian's dad yelled. "Those logs look pretty dangerous."

Naomi's voice rose in panic. "What are you looking for?"

Sonny Dille stumbled back up the beach to where Naomi and Ruth stood. "Brian thought he saw Jess's sportsbag hanging on a piece of driftwood out on the island when we were out here earlier. Whatever was there is gone." Sonny wiped his hands with his bright red handkerchief. "I'm pretty confident. We've got both of Jess's socks. She's one smart young woman. Ernie and she can't be far from here."

"But not in the river. Please, not in the river," Naomi cried into the wind.

Brian climbed onto a rock at the end of the spit that stretched into the current, held his dad's binoculars to his eyes, and searched the tossing, roaring, silver-and-brown river for signs of life. He wished he could see around the bend.

25. Ernie in the Boat

"My feet are wet." Ernie was pouting. "I think we should go home now." His head hurt and his throat was sore and he was confused. Why was he out in a boat? He didn't remember this lake. A lake is a body of water, but this could not be a lake, because it was running somewhere. There was a fast current. Lakes don't have currents in them. The ocean has currents. He must teach his class about the Labrador current and the Gulf Stream. But where was his class? Ever since Ruth's cousin, the young Olnichuk boy had drowned, he hadn't been able to talk about the world and its water systems. Let alone go fishing.

Where was Ruth? Why was he with this girl? He didn't like this boat much. It wasn't safe. Not like his canoe.

Ernie lifted the tin cup out of the water,

touched its cold rim to his lip. He put the cup down on his lap and stuck his right hand under his left armpit to warm it, but his body did not feel warm. It felt nothing. His clothes were damp and the fabric stiff with something. Ruth should wash these things. Where was she? Why wasn't she here with him? She wouldn't fit in the boat with this kid in it.

"Is this a field trip? Where are the rest of the kids?"

The girl pushed her blond hair away from her eyes, tilted her head to the left, and smiled at him.

He wished he remembered her name. One of the brochures about his disease said that names were one of the first things to go. He'd had to give up on names. Call people something else, sweetie or dear or fella or princess. Ernie let a small smile creep across his face. He was remembering a list of names to call people. It was a small victory. Maybe they wouldn't guess his secret. Maybe he could hide the truth.

He coughed so hard he nearly dropped the cup. He wiped his nose on his sleeve. He wished he was home. Why was he here?

This chill, this fever, all the aches and pains worried him. Would Ruth make him go to a hospital? If he went to a hospital, he mightn't get out. He would become a prisoner. He had seen the locks on the doors in that place. Some place that he ran from. That's how he had gotten here, to the river. He had been running away to the river. He had been planning a trip. Just him and God. Only now he was with a young girl with blond hair in her eyes and worry wrinkles on her brow.

Didn't she know this boat wasn't big enough, strong enough, for a trip down a raging river? He was already soaking wet from the spray. Wasn't that a log floating past? Not a good idea, this trip. He should speak to her about it.

"Do I know you, princess?" he asked. "God's waiting for me at the end of this road, you know. It's really nice of you to take me for this ride down the river. But this boat. It isn't safe." And he let his hand trail in the water again, felt the cool smoothness of the water flowing over his stiff old fingers, felt the sun drying his hair, the light breeze blowing against his cheek. He let the stillness of the river valley reach inside to his heart. The old ticker had had to work mighty hard lately and he didn't know how much more it could take. He felt the water flowing over his hand and loved the trees rushing by on the banks and the lone hawk circling ahead over the island. He wanted to touch the feathers of that solitary bird in flight. For a fleeting moment the fog in his head rolled back like a scudding cloud in a prairie sky and he knew that he could carry on. There was God and Ruth and this young princess who was rescuing him. He would lean on them, trust them with what remained of his life.

"The Gulf Stream flows all the way to England. Did you know that, princess?"

26. Jess Gives Her Best

J ess pulled with all her might, urging the boat through the waves. She didn't answer Ernie. She didn't know where his head was, and the Gulf Stream was not important when she was trying to row to safety on the Athabasca. She bowed her head, and pulled the wimpy plastic oars through the waves. The current was carrying them towards Landis, but she couldn't steer. She had been trying to get closer to shore, over to the calmer water, the shallower side, in case of real troubles. Her shoulders, ankle, and knee ached. Her foot throbbed. She was shivering with cold.

"I shouldn't have done this. I don't think I can go on." She rested on her oars for a minute, then put her head down on her crossed arms. That's when she noticed how high the water inside the boat was getting.

"Ernie, you've got to bail. The boat is filling up with water." Maybe there was a hole in the bottom, a hole that was letting the air out and the water in. The boat would sink. Then she would have to swim for it. She shuddered.

"Ernie, do you remember how to swim?"

"I can't do up my life jacket, princess. You'll have to do it." He sat in the front of the boat staring at her, dipping water out of the boat slowly, too slowly.

"I can't reach you from here. The boat would tip." What a ridiculous conversation. They were about to drown and she was talking to Ernie as if he understood her. "Ernie, don't stand up. Don't."

He flung his half-pulled-up body back into the boat. It tipped to the left side, letting in more water.

Jess leaned forward, grabbed the cup, and started bailing like mad.

She would have to keep the boat from going under.

"Are you sure you know what you're doing, princess?"

Jess leaned to her task, tears of fear running down her cheeks mingling with sweat. "I don't want to fall in the water. I don't want to fall in the water."

A giant tree root loomed ahead of the boat. Jess grabbed her oars and pulled towards the left, away from it, towards the bank. Ernie clutched the sides. He was silent.

Jess ducked as the boat rammed the trunk of the tree. The boat was flung to the left. The root squealed as it rubbed against a large rock, dislodged, and disappeared in the current.

The boat righted itself, but it was listing. Several centimeters of cool water filled the bottom. The sides weren't as solid as they had been when they started the journey. Air must be leaking out of the boat.

The river wasn't deep here. Jess could see the boulders rocking in the current. With any kind of luck they'd be able to walk to shore. The water was cold but not icy. It was risky, but did she have an alternative?

"We may have to swim." Jess stared towards the shore, looking for a likely place to head. They were coming around a bend in the river. Jess could see the TV tower a long way ahead. Please, let that be close to town, close to safety. "Do you remember how to swim, Ernie?"

"Hang onto the boat, Jess. Hang on." Ernie shouted over the sounds of the river and the wind. "It's one of of our rules."

Thank goodness, Ernie was back. Her Ernie was back. Jess let her body roll over the collapsing vinyl side and slide into the water, grabbed a hold of the part of the boat that was still inflated, clamped her mouth shut to block the roaring river from her lungs. She hung on for dear life as the cold hit her body, and she began half-swimming, half-walking across the current, pulling the boat. In her dream her lungs had filled and she had gone down in the depths, and only waking saved her. But this was no dream.

"You all right up there?" Ernie called.

Glancing back, Jess could barely see his head and the scrawny body, now without a life jacket at all, bobbing. How could she keep Ernie safe without a life jacket? She tried to clear the water out of her eyes to see the shore. Some bright colours dancing on the shore. So far away. So impossible to reach. She was getting exhausted. Her arms ached.

Jess heard a roaring in her ears like Niagara Falls. She drew a big breath. She looked to the left, to the right. What was that noise? She hadn't thought about rapids. Could there be rapids between here and Landis? But Pete and Ernie had paddled it.

"Are there rapids, Ernie?" But Ernie couldn't hear her.

Small waves came at them from all sides. Emerging from behind an island came a jet boat, its motors roaring, someone leaning over the side, yelling.

As she strained to see ahead she caught a glimmer of green like her mother's scarf and someone standing in the water to their waist. Whoever it was, was waving frantically. A little cluster of people gathered on the river bank. They were jumping up and down. Was that her family? Jess felt tears gather. She pulled frantically towards the shore with her free hand, but the current pulled the boat downriver. Where was the jet boat? The water was so, so cold. She couldn't feel any pain in her legs, just numbness. Then the jet boat's motors beat and thudded in her ears as it pulled past the struggling pair — for a moment Jess worried that they were going away — and then the sleek boat turned and came back, slowing to the speed of the current.

Ernie waved from his end of the half-submerged boat. "God has come to rescue me." His face was suffused with light. "Help me, help me!"

Jess clutched the boat, screamed at the rescuers. "You'll have to pull him in, his left side doesn't work."

As the jet boat came alongside, the waves buffeted the inflatable. The smell of the gas and fumes filled Jess's nose. She choked and sputtered. A hand reached down for her.

"Take Ernie first," she shouted. "He's lost his life jacket."

Jess felt the drag of the powerful motors, saw the turbulent waters, watched through water-filled eyes as burly arms reached down for Ernie, slipping a harness over his head, pulling him up out of the inflatable. She felt the sudden collapse of the ridiculous water-filled sinking boat, and she let go, let the damaged boat go, and gave her whole attention to battling the river. A long pole and arms reached down to her. She heard her name being screamed from the shore. She looked up into the rescuer's eyes and shook her head, turned her weary soaked limbs towards the beach, and began to half-swim, half-clamber towards her family.

"What is Jess doing?" Holly cried.

"She's headed for shore," Mark hollered back.

Everyone on shore screamed and yelled.

Sonny Dille waded out to join his son in the whirling current closer to Jess. Brian reached out his hand to her as the current and the waves sent her hurtling downstream. Her body rose and fell in the waves. Her arms flailed.

Brian strained into the wind and the waves. His father gripped Brian's right hand tightly as they made a human chain into the raging torrent. Naomi and Ruth joined them, allowing Brian to move further into the current.

Jess bobbed up and down. Her mouth was full of water. She coughed and spluttered. At the last moment as the current threatened to bear her away, her foot touched solid ground, her hand reached out, and she felt Brian Dille's firm grip. He tugged her to shore, her body jarred by rocks and boulders.

Jess struggled onto the rocks and fell into the outstretched arms of her mother. They stayed frozen in a hug, sobbing on each other's shoulders, water streaming from Jess's hair, her torn jacket and ruined jeans. Ruth wrapped them in blankets from the four-by-four.

"You did it, son! You did it!" Sonny grabbed Brian and hugged him so tight Brian could feel the pressure all the way to his heart. Brian shivered and shook, water streaming down his cheeks, as Ruth wrapped blankets around him and his father. Every muscle he owned screamed with exhaustion.

The jet boat's motor slowed and two lumberjacks used poles to keep the boat from foundering on the rocks or moving downstream away from the shivering crowd on the beach. Ruth watched from the shore, water lapping over her sneakers. "Ernie are you all right? Why doesn't he answer me?"

Holly waved from the cockpit of the boat and steered close enough to throw a line around a tree that hung over the river. The TV crew leaned out, cameras rolling.

The two guys let down a small dinghy. One paddled across for Ruth. She climbed in, loaded down with her purse, the first aid kit from Sonny's car, and two more blankets.

"Keep him warm till I get there. He gets colds and flu so easily. How is he? Is he hurt?"

The TV crew stood by the prow taking pictures. Mark hollered. "We've got it all!"

"Okay, that's enough!" Sonny Dille hollered. "You guys can go back to the city now. This story is over. Jess is exhausted. Leave us alone."

Mark shrugged his shoulders and turned away. The TV guys just kept rolling footage. Brian wanted to yell at Mark, tell him it was all right, that his dad was upset, that suddenly there on the beach all the anxiety of the last few days was stacked like a pile of driftwood. None of them seemed to be able to move.

Two people were coming to shore in the dinghy.

"What about the kid?" Holly's dad hollered from the deck. "We could take Jess."

"I'm not letting her out of my sight!" Naomi shouted, her green scarf sliding to the ground, making Jess giggle uncontrollably. She bent and picked the scarf up. Her mom was just the same. All this time and her mom was just the same. Jess leaned against Naomi, smelling the oh-so-familiar, wonderful smell of good shampoo and aloe vera skin lotion. Jess clutched the green paisley silk scarf in her hand as if it were a life preserver. She didn't want to move.

Brian watched as Ruth disappeared with Mark and Holly. Ernie would be safe now. Jess was struggling up the beach, her blond hair soaked and tangled, her jacket torn, a soggy sweater wrapped around her, one knee oozing blood, dragging one foot, bare, swollen, and scratched, putting all the weight on the other squishing in a wet sneaker.

A woman from the TV crew and a camera man caught up to them by the four-by-four.

"We need to get Jess to the hospital." Brian's dad started the car. "You can wait for your interviews."

"Just one question, Jessie," the newswoman leaned against the door of the four-by-four. "Why

194

did you go?"

Jess shook her head and let the drops of water from her head cascade to the ground. "Ernie needed me. When he started to drive away in his camper, I went with him — to keep him safe." She shuddered, thinking about the bear and the river and the storm. "Ernie got hurt in the crash," Jess's teeth chattered. "He's got a fever. He was getting real sick. I had to bring him down the river."

"I can't believe you came down the river," Brian said. "You hate rivers."

"I know. I don't know how I did it either." Jess stared at the roaring current and shook her head. "I was just trying to save Ernie."

"It's a good thing you did. You're a hero, Jessie Baines," the anchorwoman said. "Your story has gone all around the world. Where are you going now?"

Jess stared around her at her mom, Brian and his father, and down at her hands still clutching her mother's paisley scarf. "Home."

"We have to check into the hospital first, young lady." Sonny Dille shifted into gear.

The TV woman leaned on the open window, the camera man close beside her. "Perhaps Jess would like to make a statement for the news."

"No. That's enough," Naomi spluttered. "Let's get out of here, Sonny."

"You guys have no right pestering Jess. She's just been through a horrific ordeal," Sonny fumed. He backed the car around so he could drive up the hill.

"We haven't had a chance to talk to the rescuer. What's your name, kid? Are you Jess's boyfriend, or what?" The woman hollered questions after them as Sonny sped away. "How did you know where to look?"

Jess and Brian looked at each other.

"What were you doing here?" Her voice rasped.

Brian shrugged. "I was worried."

"Did you spot my 'crumbs,' Hansel?" Jess didn't know whether to laugh or cry. "How did you figure out where we were?"

"I saw your sportsbag in the river, scared the bejeebers out of me it did...and the sock by the school. I thought you were drowned."

"The bear took the bag, that's all."

"That's *all*? What bear? He might have attacked. You could have been mauled."

"You've always been an awfulizer."

"I know. But I came, didn't I? I didn't run away. I wanted to say thanks to Ernie before it's too late. I wanted to say, we're friends whether you like it or not. I'm not leaving for anything." Brian clamped his mouth shut. He could feel his eyes stinging and it wasn't from the river water that had soaked him.

Brian's dad and Naomi took turns telling Jess how great Brian had been, coming to the house, talking his dad into making the trip, spotting the sportsbag.

"It's thanks to this young man that you got

rescued from the river, young lady," Naomi said. "He deserves a medal."

Jess turned and glanced back at Brian. He had curled in the trunk portion of the four-by-four behind Naomi. Knobby knees stuck out of his torn jeans.

"Thanks," she said slowly. She could feel a big weight disappearing, like a rock she had been carrying had been thrown away. "Thanks a lot. You aren't bad, for a boy."

"Are you driving slowly for some reason?" Naomi leaned across from the passenger seat and tapped Sonny's shoulder. "I guess having something scary happen makes all of us slow down and smell the flowers."

"Sorry." The car sped down the road. Brian shifted position so his elbow wasn't leaning against the hard wheel well. His dad had started whistling and drumming his fingers in time with the music on the radio.

Brian could still smell the river, and the wet clothes stuck to his skin. And he was reaching for Jess, straining into the current to help her. The image of the rescue replayed and replayed. An overwhelming sense of relief made him shudder. Brian, the clown, the showoff who did things for a laugh. Who was he now? Had it only been yesterday morning that he'd tumbled in the grass to impress Jess? What a silly kid.

All of them had been on a journey — Jess and Ernie, he and his dad, and Ruth and Naomi. All of life from this point on would date from today, before the runaway and rescue and after. Who he was, who he became, would be marked by this. He didn't know how yet. He'd have to wait and see. And that was no joke.

27. Look Homeward

Jess caught herself staring at the TV tower as it drew closer, too tired, too wet to care about anything except getting warm and dry and clean, and having a cheeseburger with french fries and a piece of pecan pie with vanilla ice cream on the side and two cans of root beer. She had been aiming towards that TV tower when the jet boat and Brian had rescued them.

Neither Jess nor Brian had spoken for several kilometers. Lines of tiredness were etched on everyone's face.

Jess burrowed deeper into the car blanket and Ruth's sweater wrapped around her shivering shoulders. She just wanted to be home, safe and sound in her own house, room, bed. She had the people she loved around her, her mom and Ruth, Brian and his dad, who really cared about her, who came looking for her and Ernie. She had everything she needed.

"Too bad about your sportsbag, eh?" Brian said. He looked really relieved. His jeans were soaking wet. He'd been in the river trying to save her, in that cold river. "You'll have to buy another survival kit." Brian laughed, sounding more like his old clown self.

Jess ignored what he'd said. "The boys will think you're some softie, coming looking for me."

"I doubt it."

"Brian said this was important," Sonny Dillc glanced over his shoulder as he slowed for the junction where the road to Calling Lake met the road from Lac La Biche to Landis. "First time I've gotten this close to the land in fifteen years. I could get to like it, you know. It's not Trinidad, but...."

"You live here now, right?" Naomi said slowly. Her voice, Brian noticed was softer, more relaxed. "If you lose your family, you build a new one — like Ernie and Ruth did when their kids moved away. Like we did when Jess's dad left. We're all survivors. Keeping in touch with those who care for you is important."

"The folks in this car are getting too downright philosophical for me," Brian said, loud and clear. "This deputy sheriff votes we get this here young lady to the hospital, pack our bags, get some food, and check on Ernie so we can take the whole bunch of us back to 34th Avenue. We ought to have a party to celebrate."

28. In the Hospital

Ernie Mather lay sleeping in a high white bed with the sides pulled up. He had been bathed and dressed in fluffy blue-striped pajamas. His white hair had been blown dry and lay softly like a halo around his pink, scrubbed-looking, shaved face. He woke slowly and began plucking lint off the pale green bedspread. A bowl of silk flowers from the Landis relatives was on the side table. An intravenous tube was attached to his right arm and a machine that monitored his heart stood to the left of the bed. His left arm was in a cast. The floor was polished and the air smelled of disinfectant and cabbage. Luncheon trays clattered in the hall.

Jess stood at the door to Ernie's room, leaning on the door frame. Her mom had gone back to the Olnichuks' to pack. An ambulance was taking Ernie to the University Hospital tomorrow morning. The Mathers' family doctor had notified the specialists and they would be waiting to run tests and see how sick Ernie was.

"Hi, Ernie," she called.

"You saved his life, you know." Ruth Mather appeared beside her.

"Is that you, Ruth?" Ernie's worn-out voice called.

"It's me."

"Tell that young nurse beside you to get me some fresh water for these flowers. They're wilting."

"That's Jess, Ernie. You remember Jess, don't you? She brought you back to us."

"Have I been away a long time? Why am I in hospital? When can I go home?"

Ruth pulled up a chair and took Ernie's hand in hers. She started talking quietly.

"I'm really glad you're alive, Ernie. You know that, don't you?"

Tears filled Ernie's eyes. "Are you sure about that? I'm not myself, you know."

"Yes, you are, you are. We have great times still. I'm afraid I haven't been very honest. I thought if I didn't tell you how bad it was that you wouldn't know. That's the way they did it in the old days. The patient was the last to know." Ruth was patting his right hand, holding it up to her cheek.

"I know, Ruth. I've known for a long time."

"I realize that now. Brian told me about your files. It's hard, doing it alone. You don't have to do it alone, Ernie. I'm with you."

"You won't leave me, will you?" Ernie asked.

"I'll stay with you." Ruth's usually firm voice wavered.

"I'm not very good company. Ask the princess there. She'll tell you. I caused her a lot of grief, I think. Did I?"

Jess limped over to the bed, leaned across the clean white bedspread and planted a kiss on Ernie's freshly shaved face. She felt suddenly older than last week. Life had been pretty dramatic for her and Ernie this last few days. She had faced her worst nightmare. There had been storms, but they had come through them. She grinned at old Ernie.

"Keep singing, Ernie, remember." Jess started to sing. " 'When you walk through a storm, hold your head up high, and don't be afraid of the dark. At the end of the storm is a golden sky and the sweet silver song of a lark.' " Then Jess sang slowly as she made up a second verse, changing the words of the old familiar song to fit her and Ernie's experience. She sang about boats and water and friends at the end of the journey and the splash of an otter. Everyone chuckled.

"Thanks, princess. You sing well, you know."

"I had a good teacher."

"Enough of this silliness," said Ruth. "We'll have to have a big chicken dinner to celebrate Ernie's safe return."

"What are we celebrating now?" Ernie

asked, scratching his chin.

Jess left them and wandered down the hallway towards the waiting room, her mind churning like the waves in the Athabasca. The doctor had said she could go, that her foot was just sprained and her knee bruised, but she needed a couple of days rest, some home cooking and normal life. She bit her lip. Stupid orange socks. They'd stayed in her drawer for a whole year. Now they were lost in the Athabasca woods along with her sportsbag. Her life was full of losses. Midas was gone and Ernie was going.

Then again, she had rescued Ernie, braved the river in an inflatable, and finally, with the help of Brian, conquered the river. She wasn't sure she'd ever want to go in a boat again. She would probably play it safe for the next few years. But she would know inside that she had done what she had done. It would be enough. Jess turned into her hospital room and ran water in the sink in the corner of the room, took a fluffy white washcloth and sponged her face with warm water and soap. She wiped her hands dry with the soft towel and walked back into the quiet corridor.

Her mom, Brian, and his dad came through the swinging doors at the other end of the hall. Jess could smell the hamburger and fries the second the door opened. She dragged her bandaged foot to the grouping of green plastic chairs and table and flopped down.

"It's double cheese," Brian laughed. "The guy

at the takeout threw in a second burger and an extra piece of pecan pie when he found out who it was for. Mark and Holly are bringing doughnuts. They want an exclusive interview. Nice kids. Teenagers. They seem to get along together. We should be able to do that too — get along, you know."

Jess stared at Brian, thought about what she'd just been through, thought about Ernie and how alone he'd been and how mean Brian had been about him. She had to say something. "This is great. Thanks. But it doesn't make up for all the dumb things you've done this year."

"What dumb things?"

"Like making a joke about how I threw a ball. How I was a mess."

"When did I do that?"

"Friends don't gang up on each other and laugh."

"Honestly, I don't remember."

Jess described the day in the playground in full detail, her voice raised loud enough to startle a nurse in the corridor. "You didn't just stand by and let the bullies say things, you dolt, you added your two cents worth. You called me a mess. I may be a lot of things, but I'm not a mess."

"Boy, oh. Is that why you've been so cold all year? I thought friends were supposed to talk to each other, eh?"

"That's just for starters. Where do you come off, talking about Ernie as if he was dead? Calling him gaga? What about that?"

"Yeah, well, I wanted to talk about that," Brian sighed. "I'm sorry about that. I didn't want to lose Ernie. I sure didn't like you acting so cold. Maybe that's why I acted so stupid. I am going to see Ernie when we get home and thank him for everything. Maybe he'll let me read to him or play gin rummy, if he can. I didn't know when to stop making jokes."

"You're right. You're a clown."

"Jess? Brian?" Naomi put an arm around Jess. "You could have died, and you're arguing. Kids." She shook her head.

"It's probably shock." Brian's dad sighed. "All the little things pile up like those logs jammed on the island in the middle of the river. You have to work things out."

"Yeah, like we have, eh Dad?" Brian grinned. "Dad says he's going to talk Mom into going on vacation with us — to Banff. It would be a first. We might get to like it." Brian was feeling pretty good about the long talk he and his dad had had as they packed up at the motel. They'd worked well together over the last few days.

Jess looked at her old friends gathered around her. She started to shake. It had just dawned on her that she wasn't in any danger any more.

Brian scrunched down, tugged at his socks, felt in his pocket for his lucky coins. He really didn't mean half of the stuff he said — why couldn't Jess see that? He had a big mouth and he knew it. Maybe he could give her his lucky coins and she'd forgive him. They could start again.

"Brian's turned into the class clown. His best friends are the bullies." Jess was still upset.

"The boys laugh if a guy spends too much time with girls."

"I'm not a girl, you dolt. I'm a person."

"You're right. But a guy has to get along, make a mark."

"You think making fun at other people's expense is making a mark? It stinks."

Brian nodded. "Okay, I've got the point."

Jess unwrapped the burger and with her mouth full said, "You eat the second one, Brian. If we are back to being buddies again, like we were when Ernie took us fishing, then we need to remember to share the good as well as the bad."

"And no laughing at the way you throw a ball, right?"

"Right!"

Brian felt for the seven lucky coins in his pocket. Part of him wanted to give them to Jess, to make up for everything. Part of him wanted to save them, so he would always remember about the day he somersaulted and missed seeing his best friend disappear, because he was showing off. Maybe he could get Jess some coins of her own. His mom would probably have some with her when she came back from her trip with her girlfriends.

Jess sat licking the cheese off her fingers. "I wish I knew where the orange socks were." She was thinking they'd make a great memento. She could wash them and put them back in the drawer. Every time she opened the drawer she would remember the week Midas died and she and Ernie had taken their long journey.

"Well, that's easy," Naomi laughed. "They're in a plastic bag in my purse. They helped, even if we didn't see them right away. We'll have to nickname you Gretel. But Brian doesn't look like Hansel. He wasn't lost with you, it was Ernie."

"Everyone was a little lost," Brian's dad said wistfully. He stood smoothing the pockets on his colourful bush jacket. Brian stood beside him. It was time they drove back to Edmonton.

"Can we go now?" Ruth Mather stood in the doorway, her hands on her hips. "Or are you going to keep dissecting this whole trip and everyone on it like some bunch of frogs in a lab?"

"The voice of common sense is heard in the halls," Naomi said. Jess tossed the garbage into the plastic bucket by the door. She could see Mark and Holly coming down the hall. She'd have to give them an interview before she could leave Landis. It would give her a chance to go over everything that happened. What was it Ernie had said, way back when he was a grownup, "An unreflected life isn't worth living." Jess would have plenty of time to reflect on this adventure.

"About the sportsbag, Jess...."

"We'll wait on that, Mom. We'll wait." Jess didn't know whether she wanted another sportsbag. Maybe a smaller back pack — for just a few essentials — like her Swiss Army knife, band-aids, some scissors and coloured pens and glue, and her journal and calendar. Maybe emergency rations, her library book.

Oh, oh, hadn't she learned anything? "Life's about more than surviving, right?"

ABOUT THE AUTHOR

Mary Woodbury is a best-selling author of books for young people. Her previous Coteau Book, *The Invisible Polly McDoodle* was an Our Choice selection of the Canadian Children's Book Centre, and has also been translated into French. Her other books include *Letting Go*, *Where in the World is Jenny Parker?* and *A Gift for Johnny Know-It-All*.

Originally from Ontario, Mary lived in Newfoundland, New York, and Italy before moving to Edmonton in the late 1970s. Extremely active in the writing community, Mary helped found a book publishing house and a literary magazine, as well as the writers' guilds of Alberta and Newfoundland. She is involved in the Canadian Society for Children's Authors, Illustrators, and Performers (CANSCAIP).

She lives in Edmonton with her husband Clair and a wire-haired terrier named Rosie.

ABOUT THE ILLUSTRATOR

Ward Schell is an artist-in-residence at the Neil Balkwill Civic Arts Centre in Regina, where he teaches drawing, painting, and cartooning. Ward received his art education at the Emily Carr Institute of Art & Design in Vancouver and at the University of Regina. He recently created the colour illustration for *Thunder Ice*, another Coteau Books novel for young readers.

ACKNOWLEDGEMENTS

I want to thank Luanne Armstrong who is my first reader, Shirley Serviss for checking the facts about Alzheimer's Disease, and my husband Clair for being a picky editor and long-time friend. The Alberta Foundation for the Arts gave me a grant several years ago to work on this novel. I appreciate their ongoing support. As a manuscript it was runner-up in the 1994 Alberta Writing for Youth competition run by the Writers Guild of Alberta. Thanks go as well to Barbara Sapergia, my editor at Coteau. It's the best small publisher in the west.

COTEAU BOOKS

*If you liked **Jess and the Runaway Grandpa**,*
check out these other great Coteau books:

THE INVISIBLE POLLY MCDOODLE
by Mary Woodbury

Twelve-year-old Polly McDoodle wants to know who's responsible for the burglaries in her apartment building, and she wants to stop feeling invisible to her parents. If she solves the crime and catches the thieves, THEN will her parents finally start to see her in a new light?

MELANIE BLUELAKE'S DREAM
by Betty Fitzpatrick Dorion

You think starting at a new school is tough? Ten-year-old Melanie Bluelake has to move to the city from the northern woods. Melanie misses her friends and fights with her mom for moving her. Most of all, she misses the loving warmth of her Kŏhkom, her grandmother.